GEORGE O'CONNOR

HERA
THE GODDESS AND HER GLORY

A NEAL PORTER BOOK

First Second

New York & London

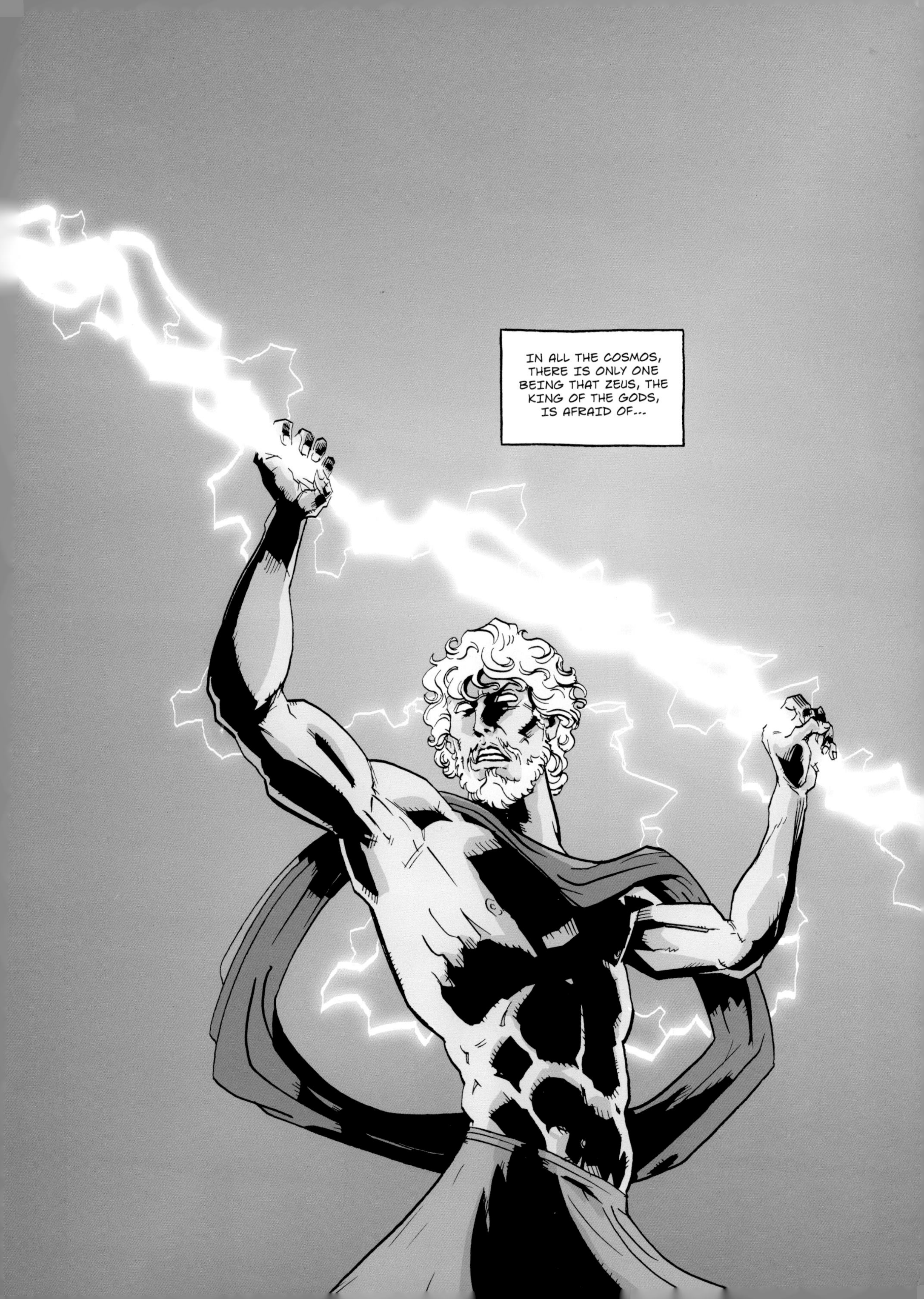
IN ALL THE COSMOS, THERE IS ONLY ONE BEING THAT ZEUS, THE KING OF THE GODS, IS AFRAID OF...

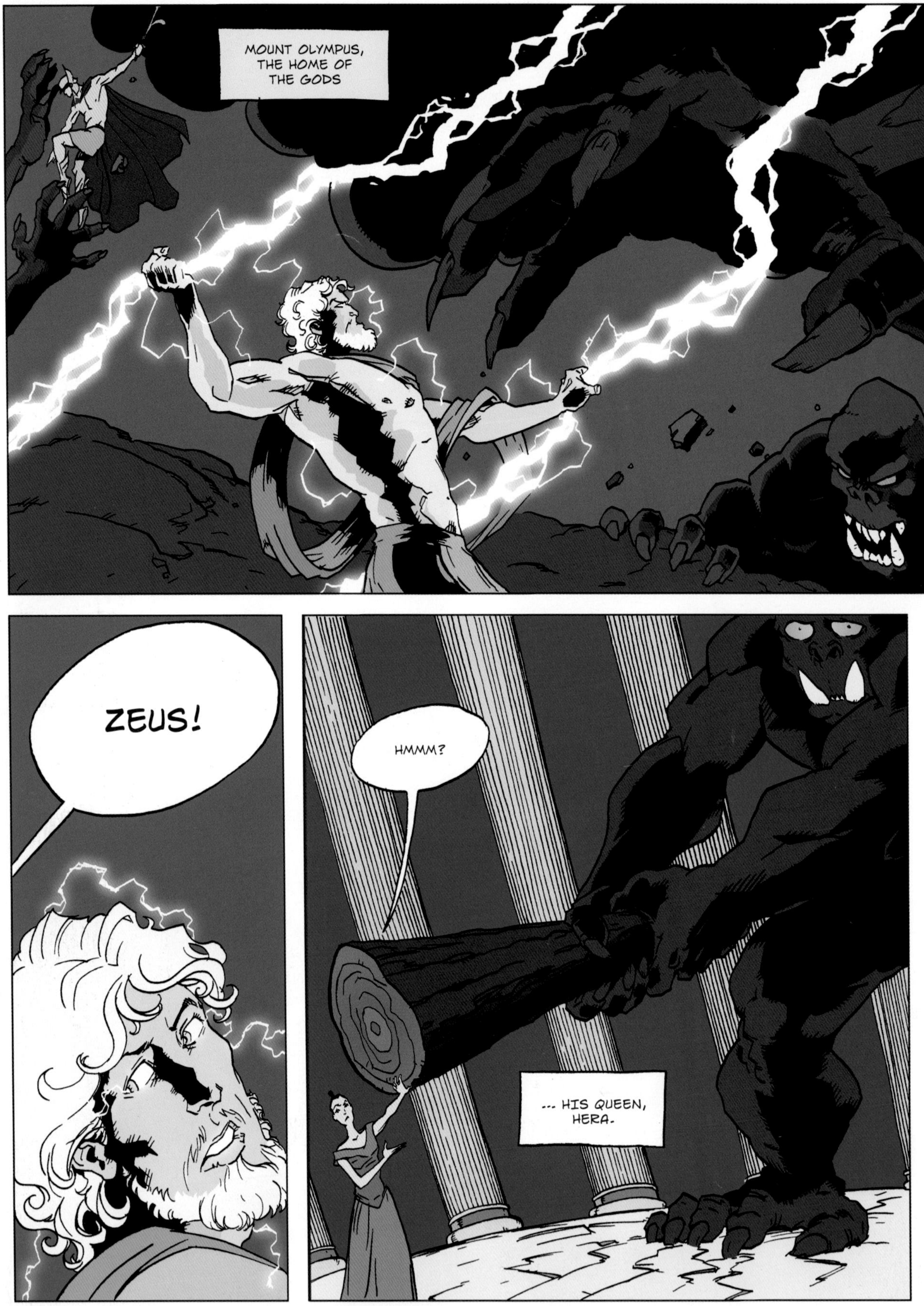
MOUNT OLYMPUS, THE HOME OF THE GODS
ZEUS!
HMMM?
... HIS QUEEN, HERA.

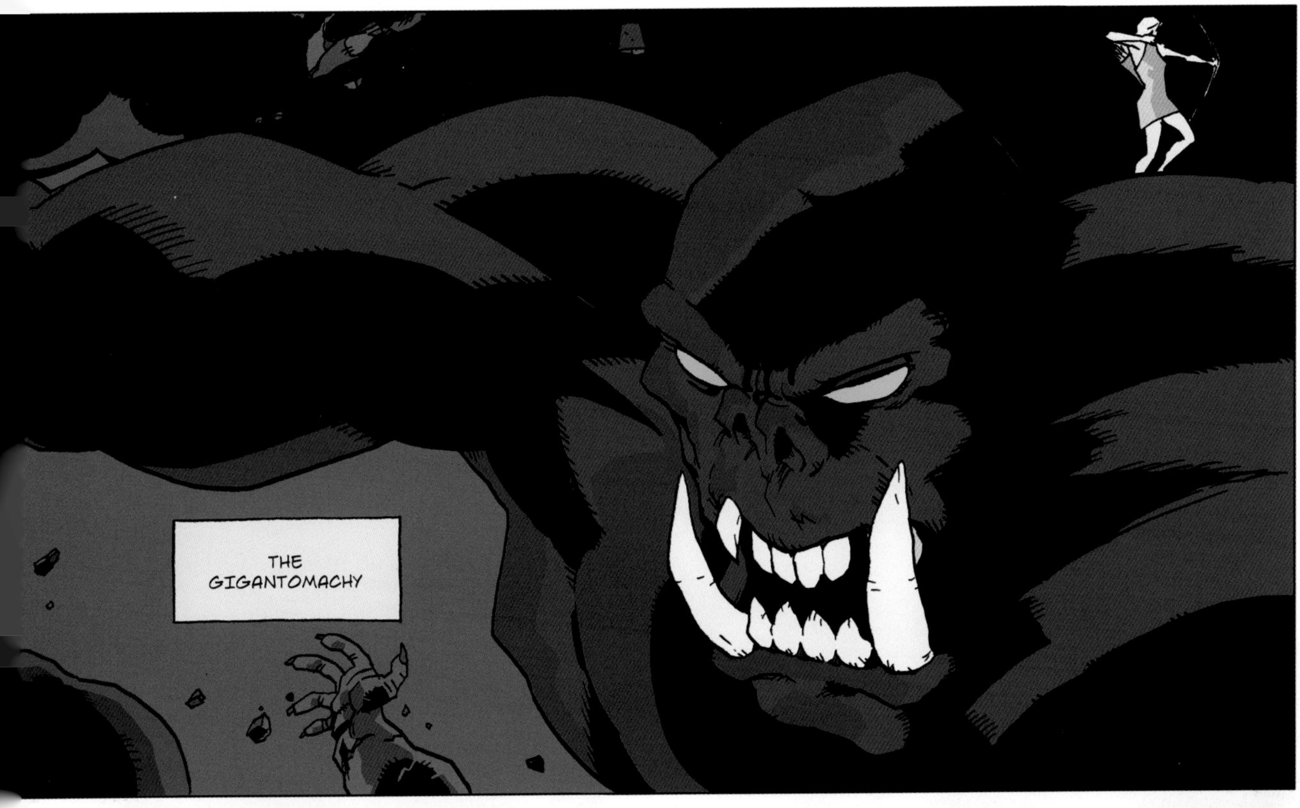
THE GIGANTOMACHY

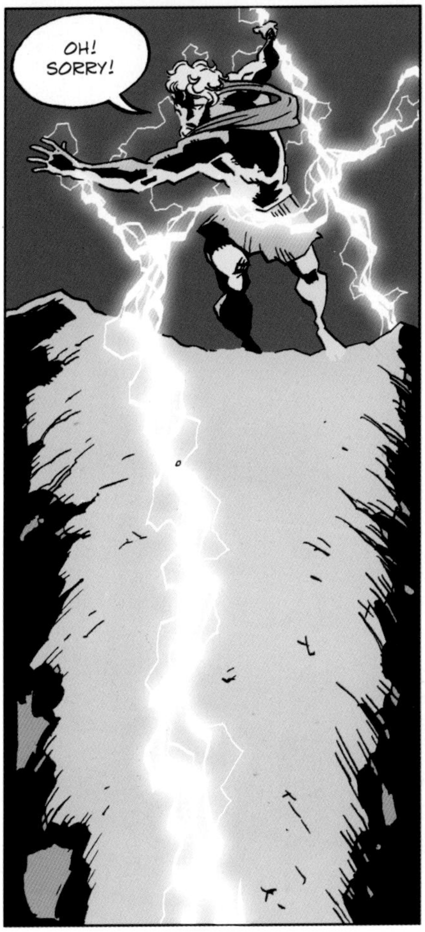
OH! SORRY!

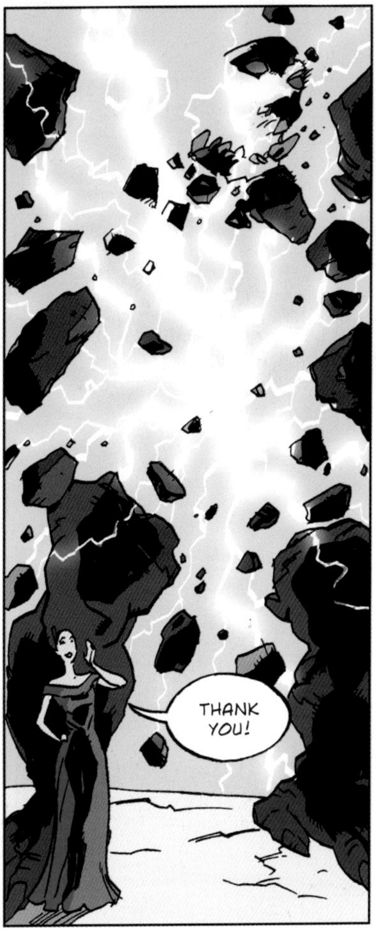
THANK YOU!

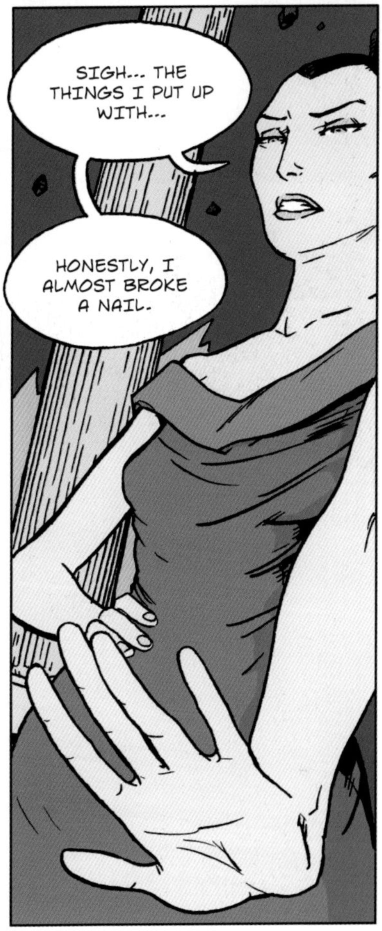
SIGH... THE THINGS I PUT UP WITH...
HONESTLY, I ALMOST BROKE A NAIL.

MANY YEARS BEFORE...

RIGHT AFTER THE OVERTHROW OF KRONOS, WHEN THE OLYMPIANS FIRST CAME TO MOUNT OLYMPUS

DON'T LOOK NOW, HERA, BUT ZEUS AND HIS NEW QUEEN, METIS, SEEM DEEP IN CONVERSATION.

... WORRY YOUR BROW, MY HUSBAND? IS THERE ANY COUNSEL I MAY OFFER?

AND HE LIKES YOU. I CAN TELL BY THE WAY HE FORGETS HOW TO SPEAK WHENEVER HE SEES YOU.

HE'S VERY CUTE...

YES, HE IS VERY HANDSOME...

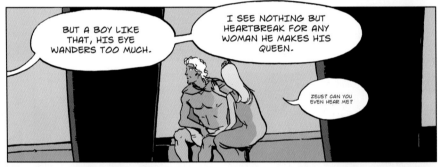

BUT A BOY LIKE THAT, HIS EYE WANDERS TOO MUCH.

I SEE NOTHING BUT HEARTBREAK FOR ANY WOMAN HE MAKES HIS QUEEN.

ZEUS? CAN YOU EVEN HEAR ME?

ONE DAY SOON AFTER, METIS DISAPPEARED, NEVER TO BE SEEN AGAIN.

IF ZEUS KNEW WHERE SHE WENT, HE WASN'T SAYING.

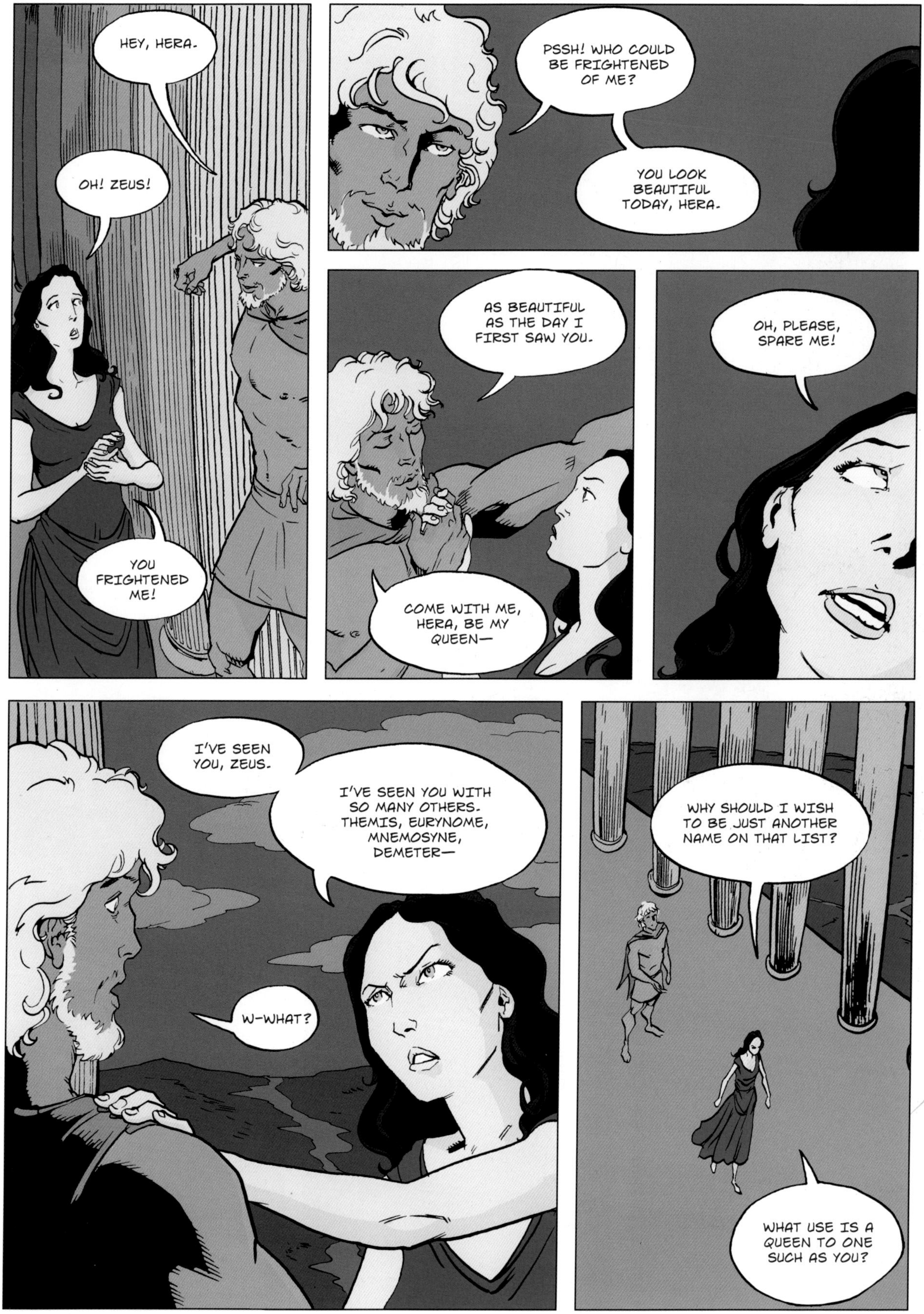
HEY, HERA.
OH! ZEUS!
YOU FRIGHTENED ME!
PSSH! WHO COULD BE FRIGHTENED OF ME?
YOU LOOK BEAUTIFUL TODAY, HERA.
AS BEAUTIFUL AS THE DAY I FIRST SAW YOU.
COME WITH ME, HERA, BE MY QUEEN—
OH, PLEASE, SPARE ME!
I'VE SEEN YOU, ZEUS.
I'VE SEEN YOU WITH SO MANY OTHERS. THEMIS, EURYNOME, MNEMOSYNE, DEMETER—
W-WHAT?
WHY SHOULD I WISH TO BE JUST ANOTHER NAME ON THAT LIST?
WHAT USE IS A QUEEN TO ONE SUCH AS YOU?

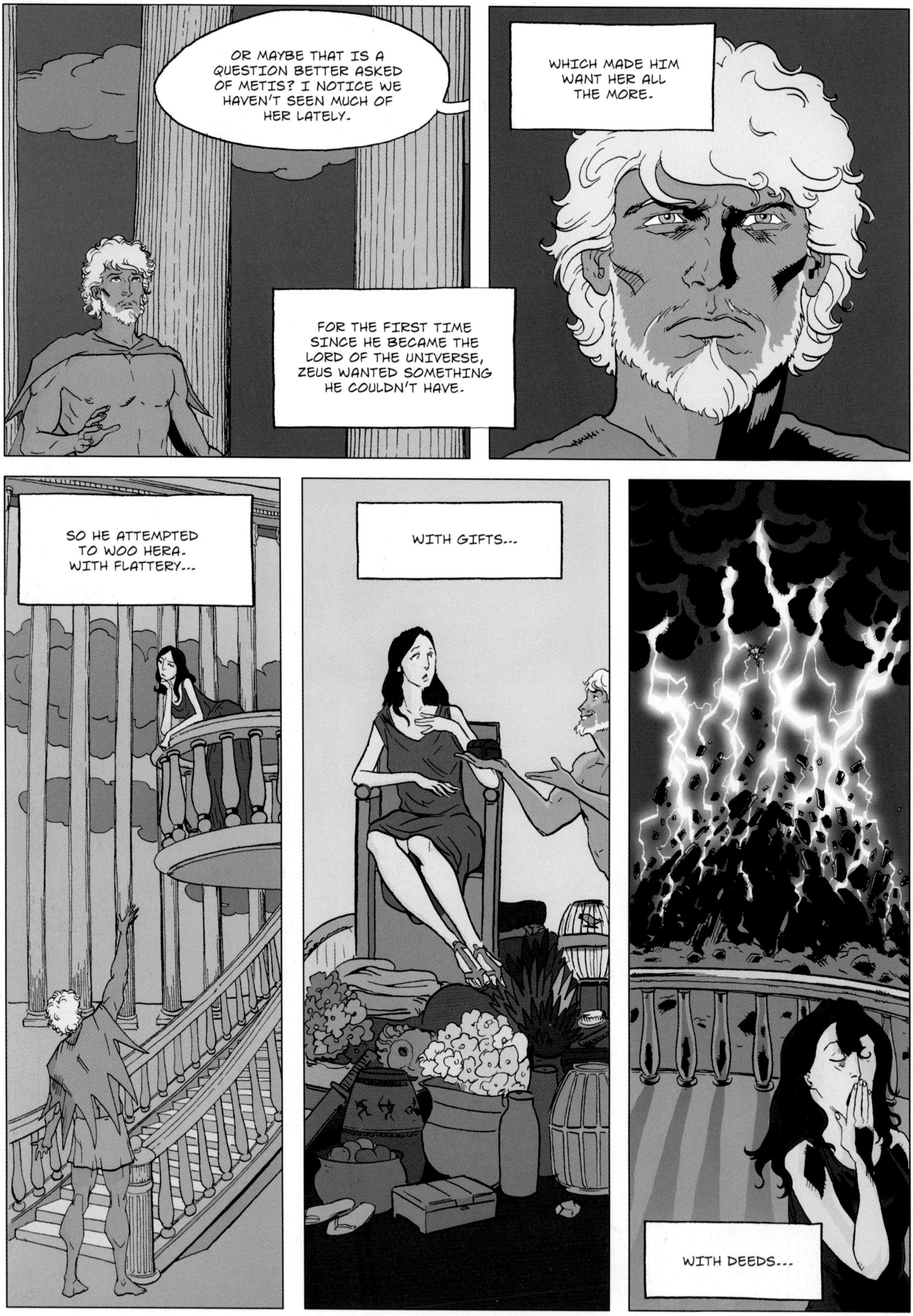
OR MAYBE THAT IS A QUESTION BETTER ASKED OF METIS? I NOTICE WE HAVEN'T SEEN MUCH OF HER LATELY.
FOR THE FIRST TIME SINCE HE BECAME THE LORD OF THE UNIVERSE, ZEUS WANTED SOMETHING HE COULDN'T HAVE.
WHICH MADE HIM WANT HER ALL THE MORE.
SO HE ATTEMPTED TO WOO HERA. WITH FLATTERY...
WITH GIFTS...
WITH DEEDS...

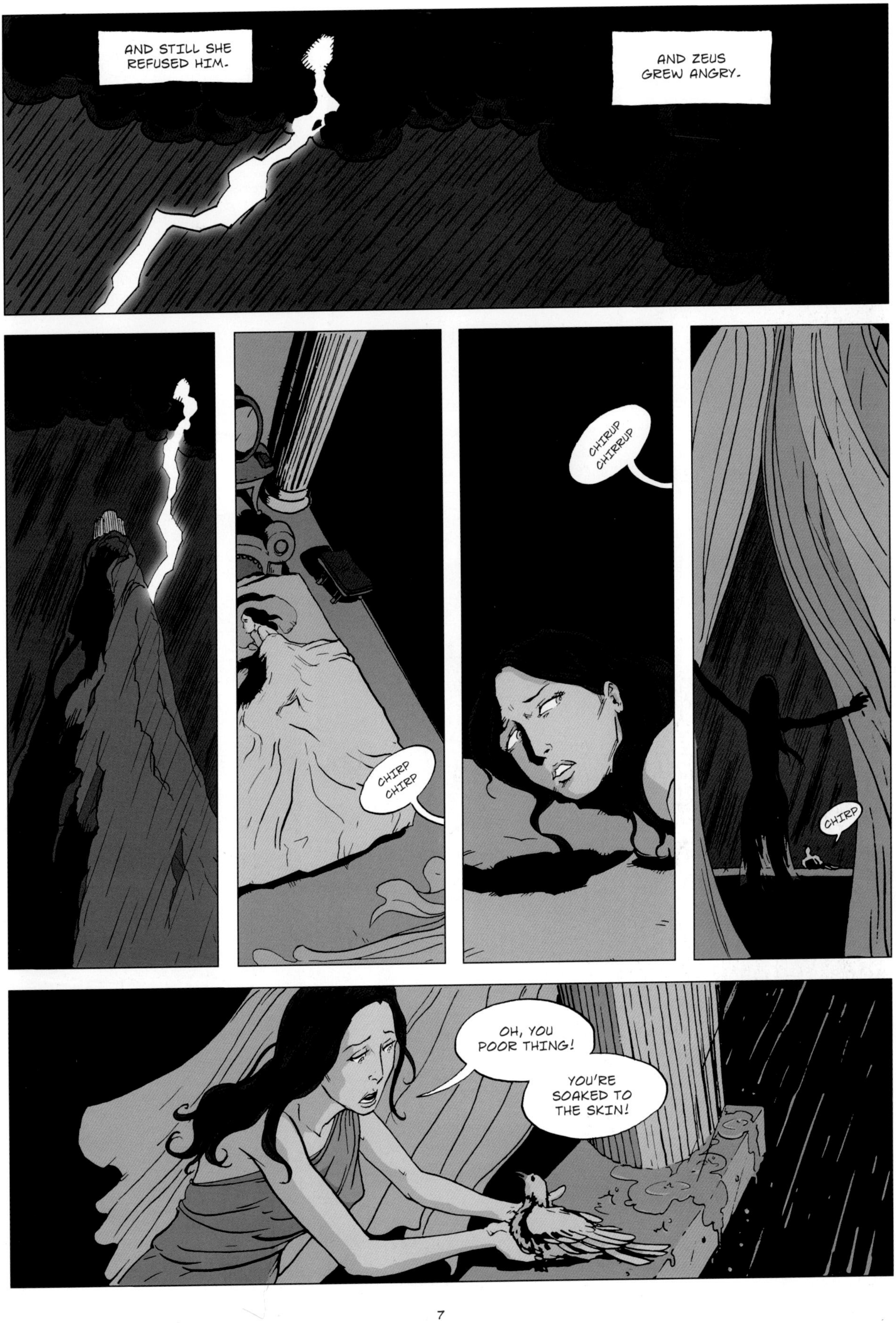
AND STILL SHE REFUSED HIM.
AND ZEUS GREW ANGRY.
CHIRP CHIRP
CHIRUP CHIRRUP
CHIRP
OH, YOU POOR THING!
YOU'RE SOAKED TO THE SKIN!

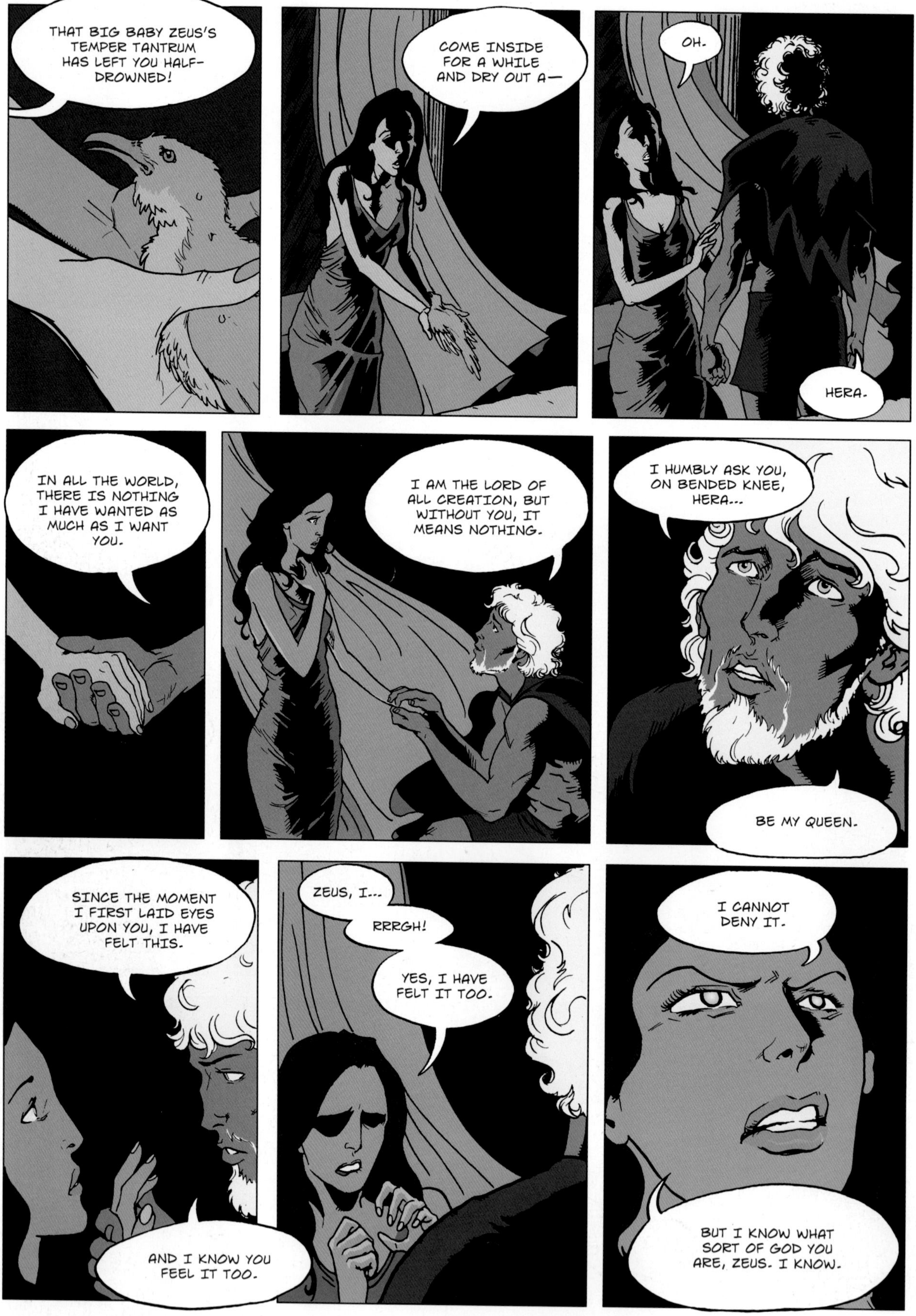
THAT BIG BABY ZEUS'S TEMPER TANTRUM HAS LEFT YOU HALF-DROWNED!
COME INSIDE FOR A WHILE AND DRY OUT A—
OH.
HERA.
IN ALL THE WORLD, THERE IS NOTHING I HAVE WANTED AS MUCH AS I WANT YOU.
I AM THE LORD OF ALL CREATION, BUT WITHOUT YOU, IT MEANS NOTHING.
I HUMBLY ASK YOU, ON BENDED KNEE, HERA...
BE MY QUEEN.
SINCE THE MOMENT I FIRST LAID EYES UPON YOU, I HAVE FELT THIS.
AND I KNOW YOU FEEL IT TOO.
ZEUS, I...
RRRGH!
YES, I HAVE FELT IT TOO.
I CANNOT DENY IT.
BUT I KNOW WHAT SORT OF GOD YOU ARE, ZEUS. I KNOW.

I WILL AGREE TO BE YOUR QUEEN.

URK!

BUT YOU WON'T JUST MAKE ME YOUR QUEEN.

I'VE SEEN HOW YOU TREAT YOUR QUEENS!

YOU'LL MAKE ME YOUR WIFE! AND ALL THAT ENTAILS.

AND WHEN I CATCH YOU WITH ANOTHER WOMAN, SO HELP ME...

AND SO IT WAS THAT ZEUS GOT WHAT HE MOST DESIRED.

AND QUITE A BIT MORE AS WELL.

ALL OF CREATION TURNED OUT FOR THE WEDDING OF ZEUS AND HERA. (FOR, AFTER ALL, IT WAS THE FIRST WEDDING. NONE OF ZEUS'S PREVIOUS QUEENS HAD NEEDED A WEDDING.)

GODS AND GODDESSES, NAIADS AND NYMPHS, CENTAURS AND SATYRS, GIGANTES AND TITANS (THOSE NOT IMPRISONED), EVEN THE PECULIAR CREATURES CALLED HUMANS. (FOR IN THOSE DAYS, THE OLYMPIANS STILL MOVED AMONG THE INHABITANTS OF EARTH.)

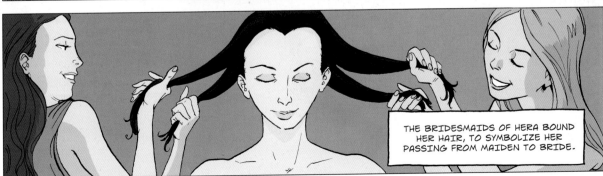

THE BRIDESMAIDS OF HERA BOUND HER HAIR, TO SYMBOLIZE HER PASSING FROM MAIDEN TO BRIDE.

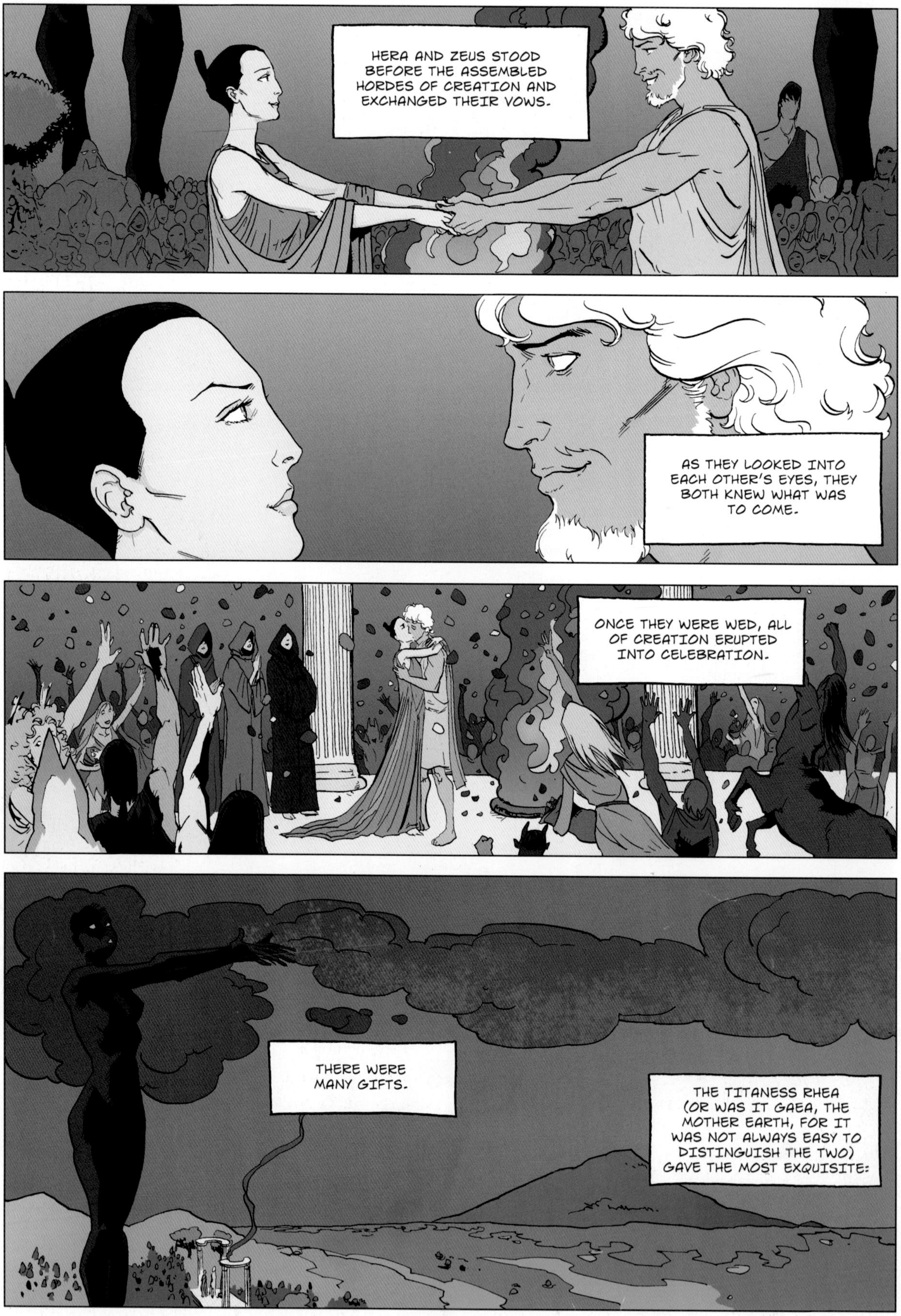
HERA AND ZEUS STOOD BEFORE THE ASSEMBLED HORDES OF CREATION AND EXCHANGED THEIR VOWS.
AS THEY LOOKED INTO EACH OTHER'S EYES, THEY BOTH KNEW WHAT WAS TO COME.
ONCE THEY WERE WED, ALL OF CREATION ERUPTED INTO CELEBRATION.
THERE WERE MANY GIFTS.
THE TITANESS RHEA (OR WAS IT GAEA, THE MOTHER EARTH, FOR IT WAS NOT ALWAYS EASY TO DISTINGUISH THE TWO) GAVE THE MOST EXQUISITE:

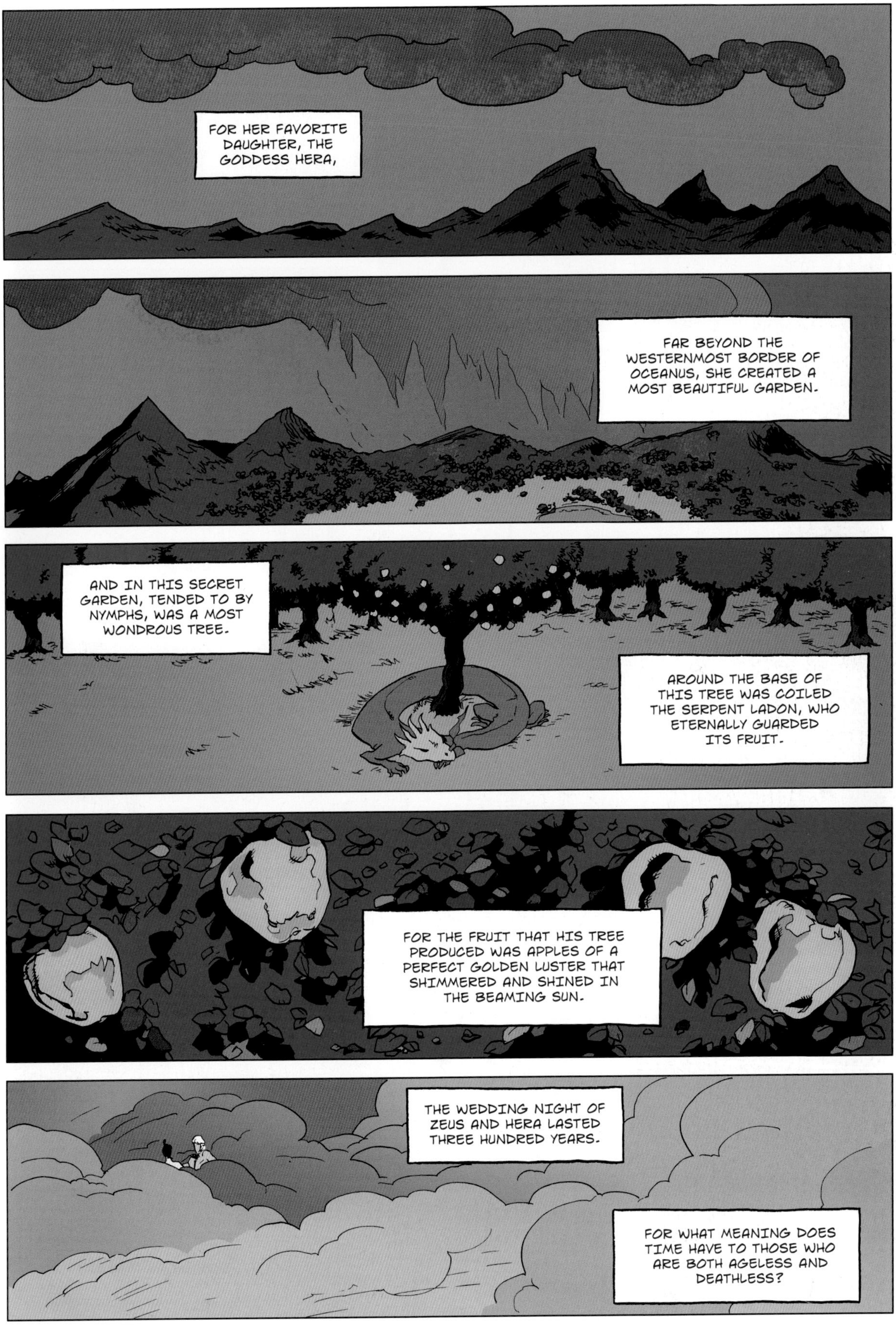
FOR HER FAVORITE DAUGHTER, THE GODDESS HERA,
FAR BEYOND THE WESTERNMOST BORDER OF OCEANUS, SHE CREATED A MOST BEAUTIFUL GARDEN.
AND IN THIS SECRET GARDEN, TENDED TO BY NYMPHS, WAS A MOST WONDROUS TREE.
AROUND THE BASE OF THIS TREE WAS COILED THE SERPENT LADON, WHO ETERNALLY GUARDED ITS FRUIT.
FOR THE FRUIT THAT HIS TREE PRODUCED WAS APPLES OF A PERFECT GOLDEN LUSTER THAT SHIMMERED AND SHINED IN THE BEAMING SUN.
THE WEDDING NIGHT OF ZEUS AND HERA LASTED THREE HUNDRED YEARS.
FOR WHAT MEANING DOES TIME HAVE TO THOSE WHO ARE BOTH AGELESS AND DEATHLESS?

THOSE THREE HUNDRED YEARS WERE THE HAPPIEST TIME FOR ALL WHO DWELLED ON THE ENTIRE EARTH.

FOR WHEN THE GODS ARE HAPPY, ALL IS HAPPY.

IN TIME, THE UNION OF ZEUS AND HERA PRODUCED CHILDREN.

BUT ZEUS FOUND THESE CHILDREN TO BE... WANTING.

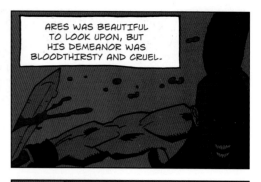

ARES WAS BEAUTIFUL TO LOOK UPON, BUT HIS DEMEANOR WAS BLOODTHIRSTY AND CRUEL.

HEPHAISTOS WAS KIND, AND AS A CRAFTSMAN CREATED WORKS OF SUCH BEAUTY AS THE WORLD HAD NEVER SEEN.

BUT HE WAS UGLY AND BRUTISH, AND HIS LEGS WERE CROOKED AND BENT.

ZEUS STILL LOVED HIS WIFE VERY MUCH, BUT, BEING ZEUS, HIS MIND BEGAN TO WANDER.

HE LOOKED OUT OVER THE WORLD AND WONDERED.

SOMEWHERE OUT THERE, IN THE VAST SPAN OF CREATION, MIGHT HE NOT FIND SOMEONE TO BEAR MORE SUITABLE CHILDREN, AS WOULD BEFIT THE KING OF THE GODS?

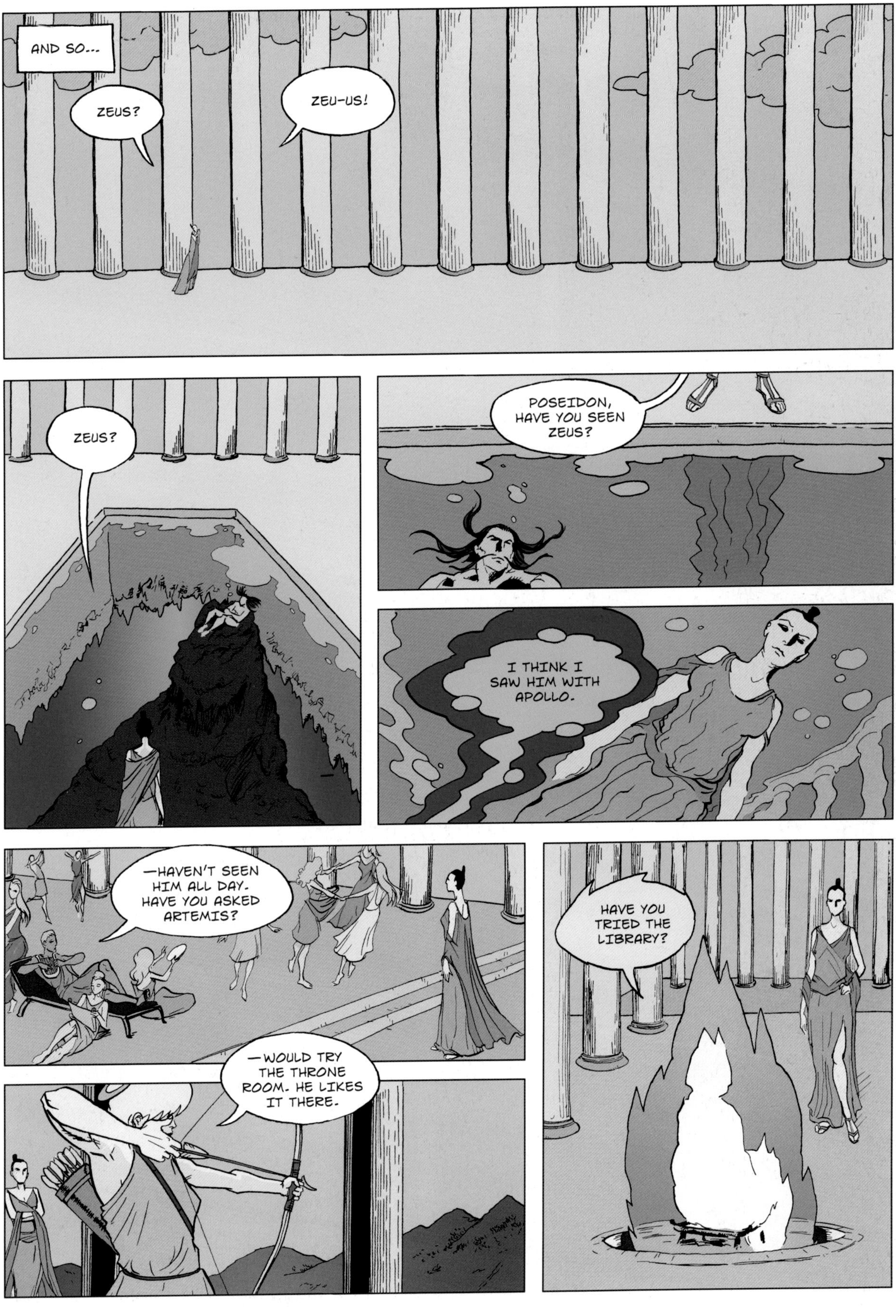
AND SO...
ZEUS?
ZEU-US!
ZEUS?
POSEIDON, HAVE YOU SEEN ZEUS?
I THINK I SAW HIM WITH APOLLO.
—HAVEN'T SEEN HIM ALL DAY. HAVE YOU ASKED ARTEMIS?
—WOULD TRY THE THRONE ROOM. HE LIKES IT THERE.
HAVE YOU TRIED THE LIBRARY?

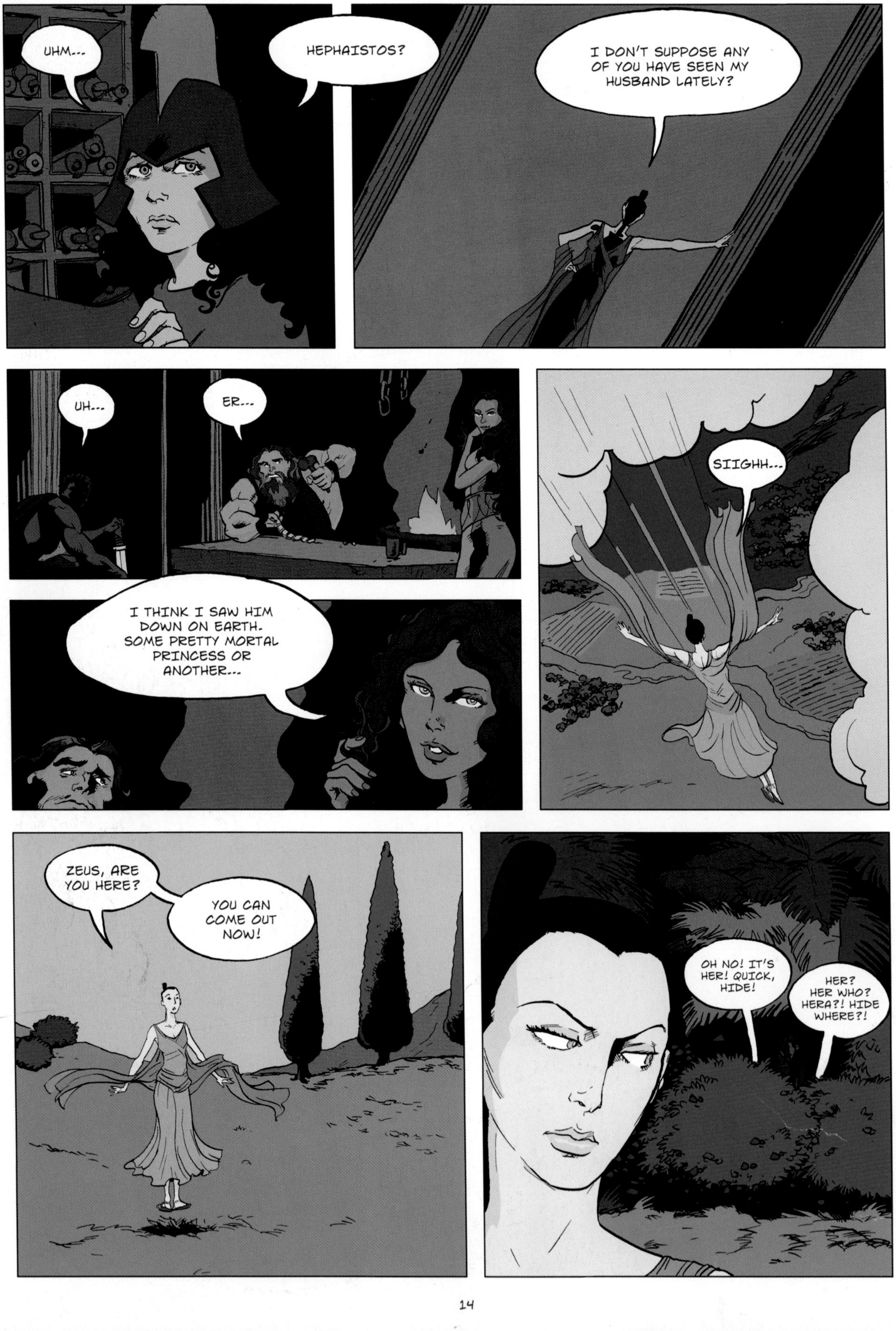
UHM...
HEPHAISTOS?
I DON'T SUPPOSE ANY OF YOU HAVE SEEN MY HUSBAND LATELY?
UH...
ER...
I THINK I SAW HIM DOWN ON EARTH. SOME PRETTY MORTAL PRINCESS OR ANOTHER...
SIIGHH...
ZEUS, ARE YOU HERE?
YOU CAN COME OUT NOW!
OH NO! IT'S HER! QUICK, HIDE!
HER? HER WHO? HERA?! HIDE WHERE?!

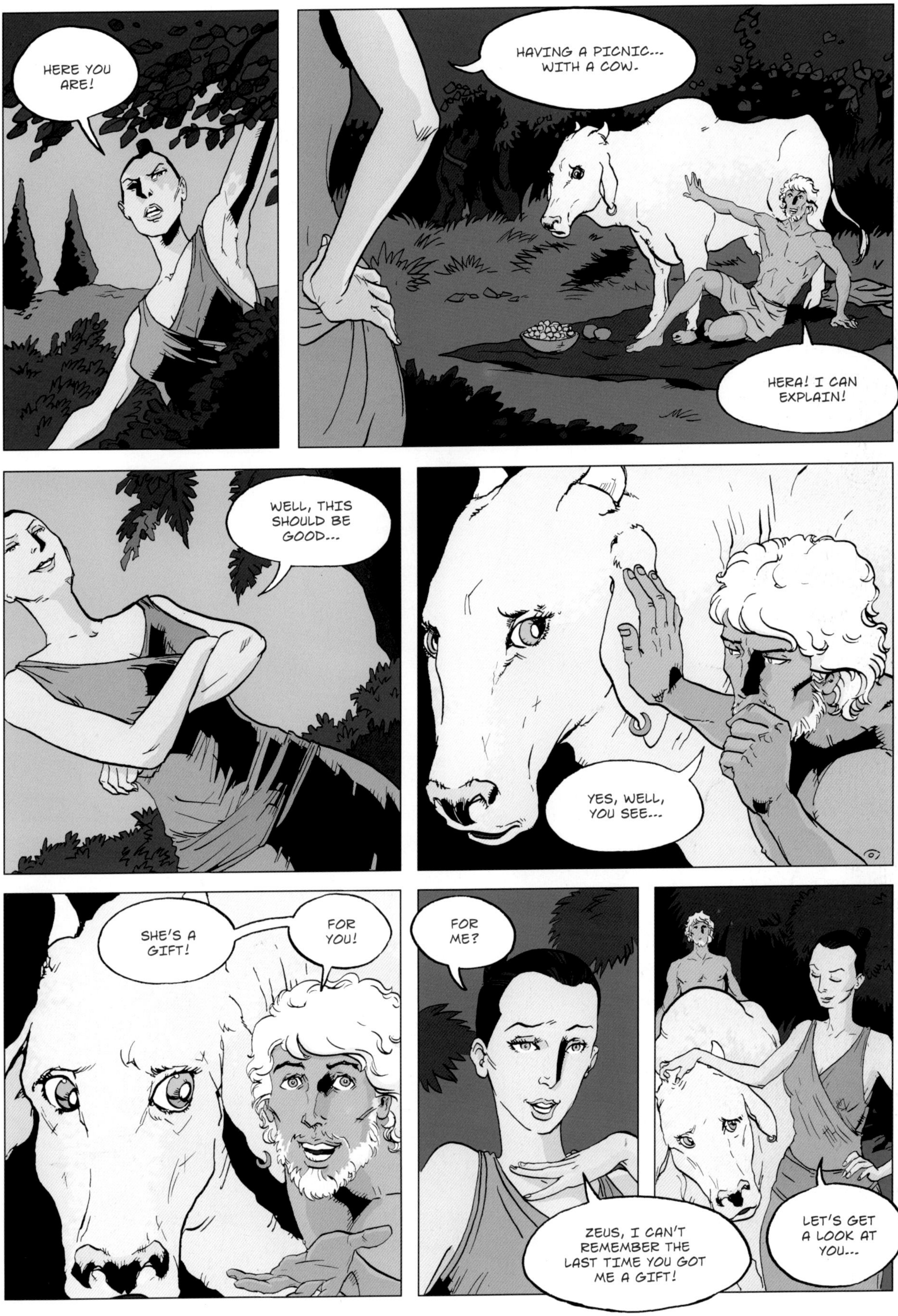
HERE YOU ARE!
HAVING A PICNIC... WITH A COW.
HERA! I CAN EXPLAIN!
WELL, THIS SHOULD BE GOOD...
YES, WELL, YOU SEE...
SHE'S A GIFT!
FOR YOU!
FOR ME?
ZEUS, I CAN'T REMEMBER THE LAST TIME YOU GOT ME A GIFT!
LET'S GET A LOOK AT YOU...

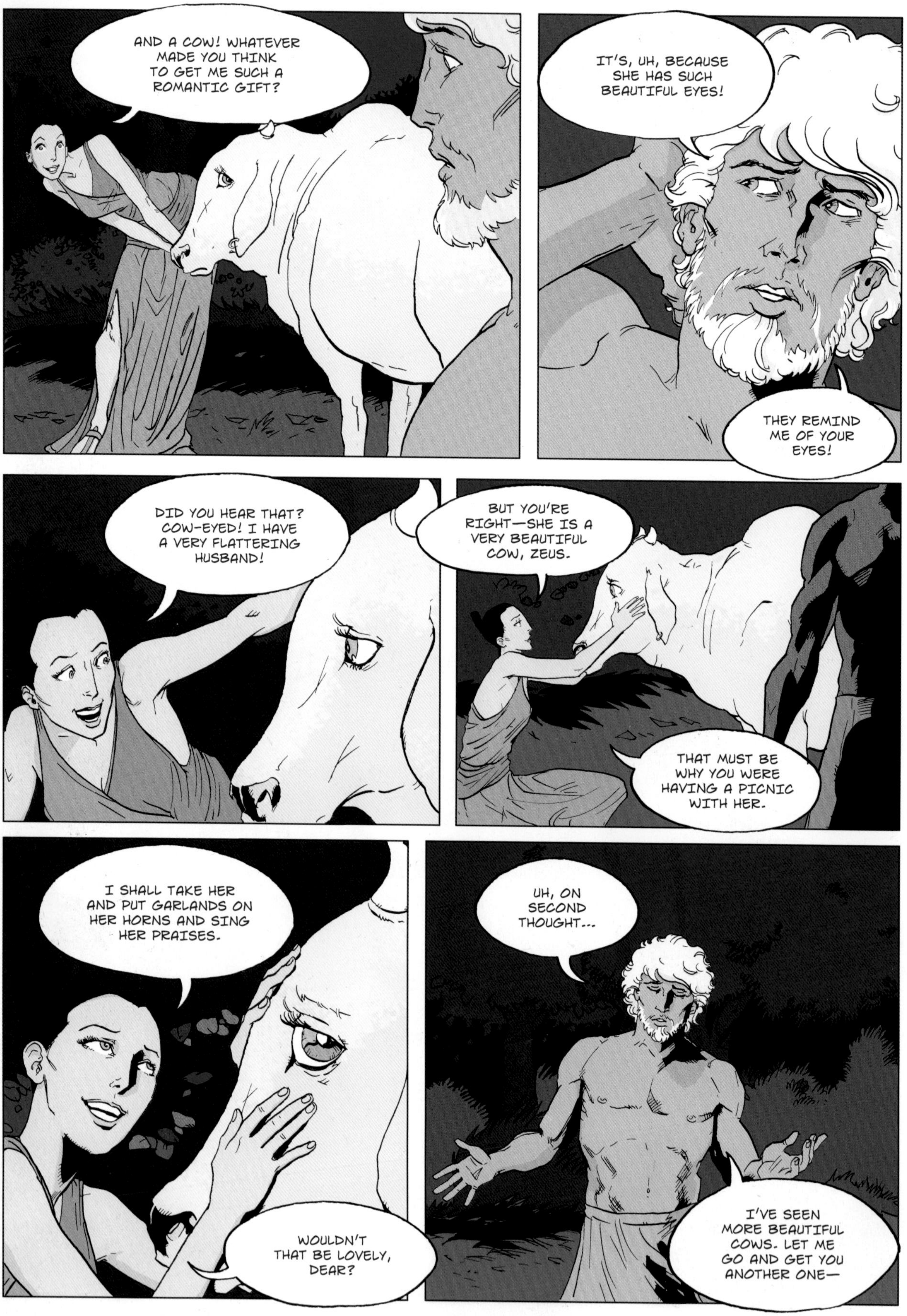
AND A COW! WHATEVER MADE YOU THINK TO GET ME SUCH A ROMANTIC GIFT?
IT'S, UH, BECAUSE SHE HAS SUCH BEAUTIFUL EYES!
THEY REMIND ME OF YOUR EYES!
DID YOU HEAR THAT? COW-EYED! I HAVE A VERY FLATTERING HUSBAND!
BUT YOU'RE RIGHT—SHE IS A VERY BEAUTIFUL COW, ZEUS.
THAT MUST BE WHY YOU WERE HAVING A PICNIC WITH HER.
I SHALL TAKE HER AND PUT GARLANDS ON HER HORNS AND SING HER PRAISES.
WOULDN'T THAT BE LOVELY, DEAR?
UH, ON SECOND THOUGHT...
I'VE SEEN MORE BEAUTIFUL COWS. LET ME GO AND GET YOU ANOTHER ONE—

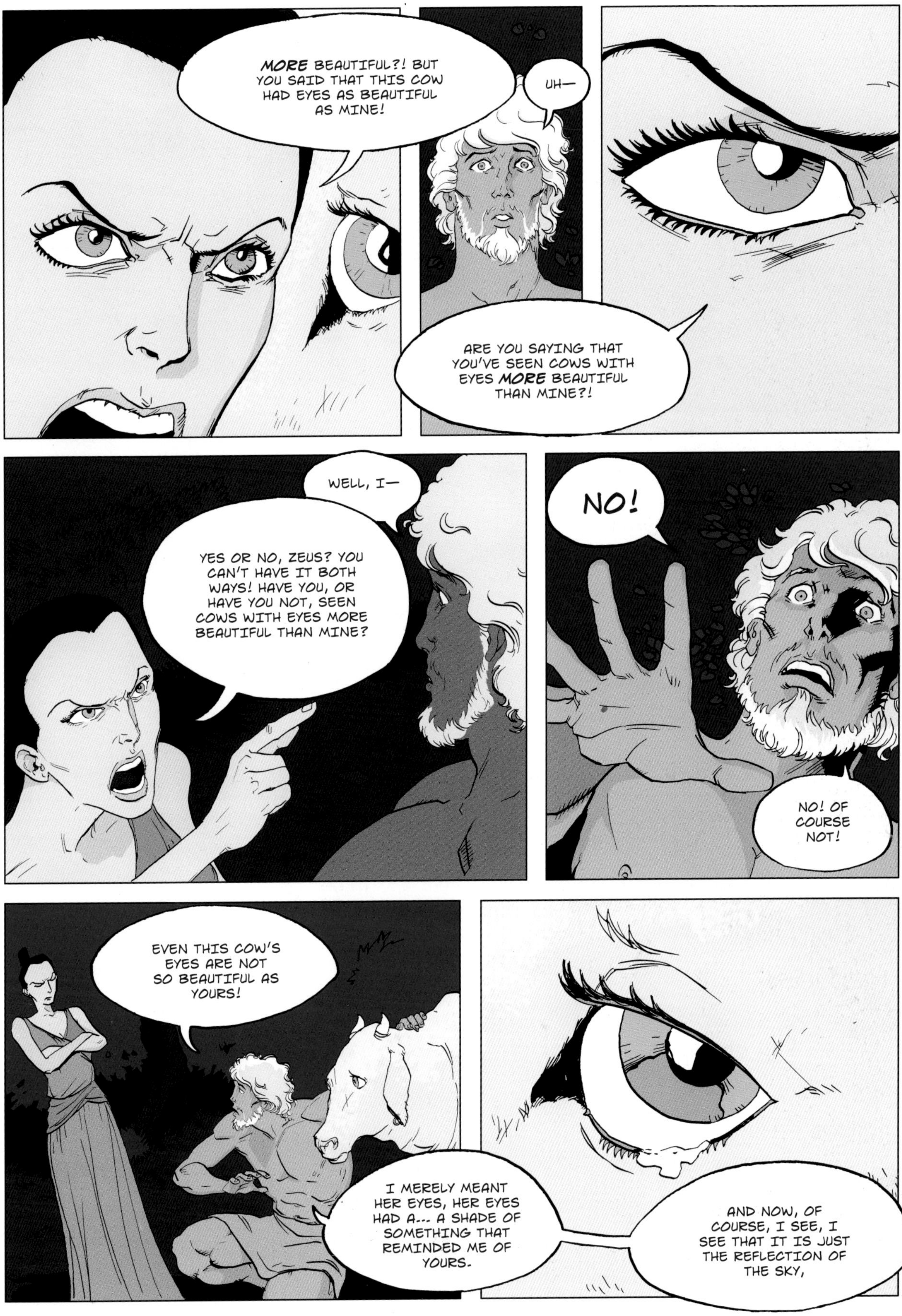

MORE BEAUTIFUL?! BUT YOU SAID THAT THIS COW HAD EYES AS BEAUTIFUL AS MINE!
UH—
ARE YOU SAYING THAT YOU'VE SEEN COWS WITH EYES MORE BEAUTIFUL THAN MINE?!
WELL, I—
YES OR NO, ZEUS? YOU CAN'T HAVE IT BOTH WAYS! HAVE YOU, OR HAVE YOU NOT, SEEN COWS WITH EYES MORE BEAUTIFUL THAN MINE?
NO!
NO! OF COURSE NOT!
EVEN THIS COW'S EYES ARE NOT SO BEAUTIFUL AS YOURS!
I MERELY MEANT HER EYES, HER EYES HAD A... A SHADE OF SOMETHING THAT REMINDED ME OF YOURS.
AND NOW, OF COURSE, I SEE, I SEE THAT IT IS JUST THE REFLECTION OF THE SKY,

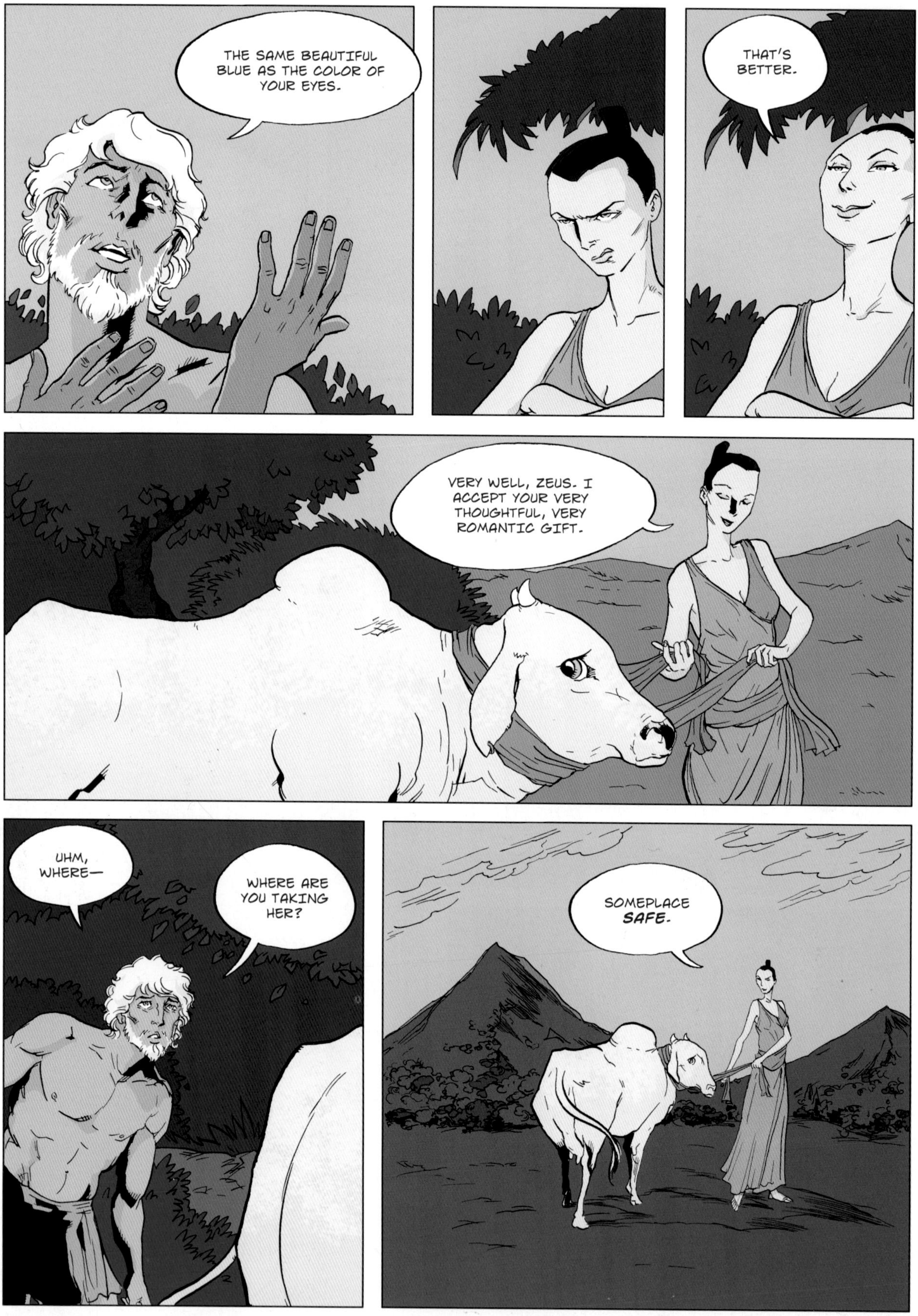
THE SAME BEAUTIFUL BLUE AS THE COLOR OF YOUR EYES.
THAT'S BETTER.
VERY WELL, ZEUS. I ACCEPT YOUR VERY THOUGHTFUL, VERY ROMANTIC GIFT.
UHM, WHERE—
WHERE ARE YOU TAKING HER?
SOMEPLACE **SAFE**.

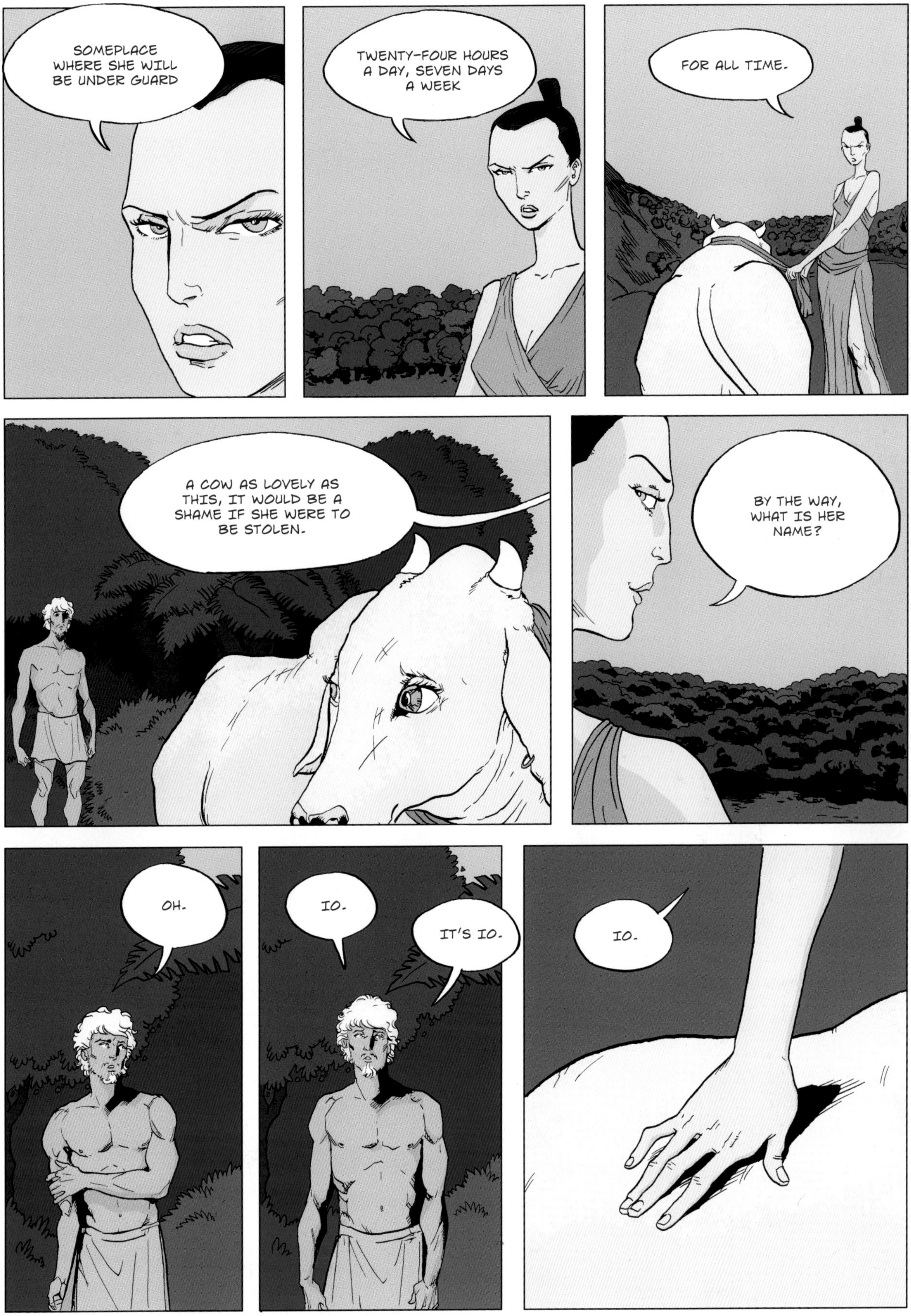
SOMEPLACE WHERE SHE WILL BE UNDER GUARD
TWENTY-FOUR HOURS A DAY, SEVEN DAYS A WEEK
FOR ALL TIME.
A COW AS LOVELY AS THIS, IT WOULD BE A SHAME IF SHE WERE TO BE STOLEN.
BY THE WAY, WHAT IS HER NAME?
OH.
IO.
IT'S IO.
IO.

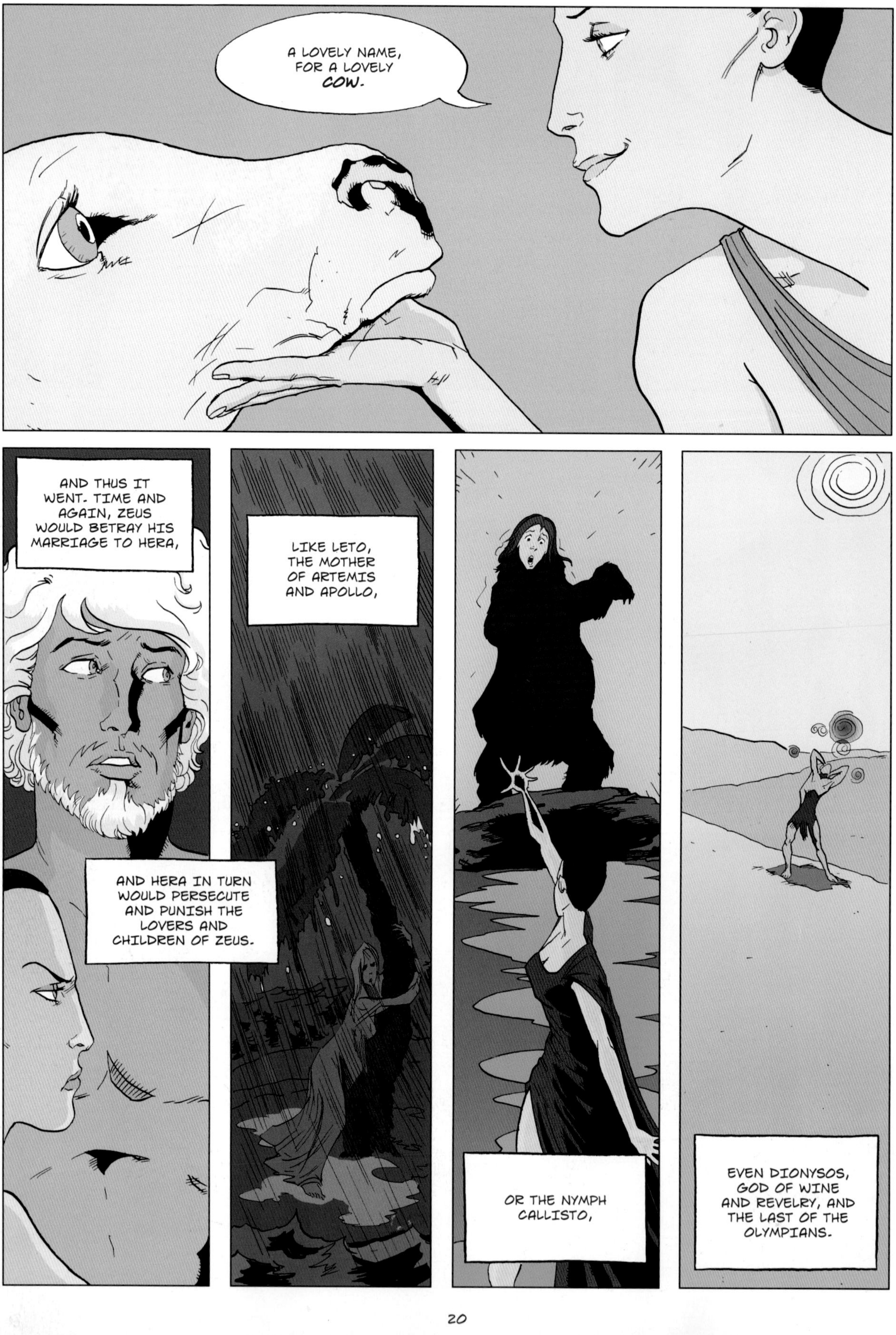
A LOVELY NAME, FOR A LOVELY COW.
AND THUS IT WENT. TIME AND AGAIN, ZEUS WOULD BETRAY HIS MARRIAGE TO HERA,
AND HERA IN TURN WOULD PERSECUTE AND PUNISH THE LOVERS AND CHILDREN OF ZEUS.
LIKE LETO, THE MOTHER OF ARTEMIS AND APOLLO,
OR THE NYMPH CALLISTO,
EVEN DIONYSOS, GOD OF WINE AND REVELRY, AND THE LAST OF THE OLYMPIANS.

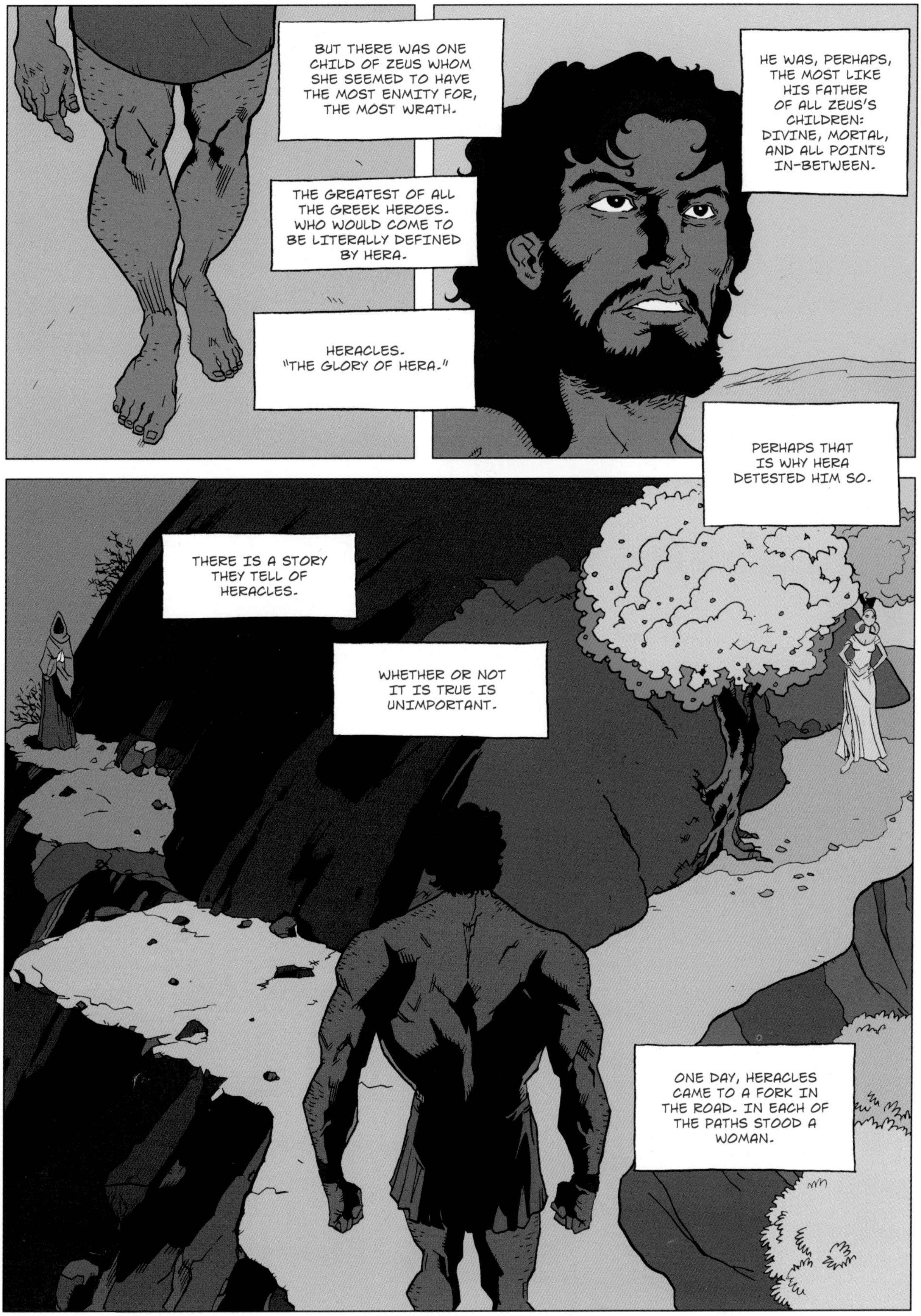
BUT THERE WAS ONE CHILD OF ZEUS WHOM SHE SEEMED TO HAVE THE MOST ENMITY FOR, THE MOST WRATH.
THE GREATEST OF ALL THE GREEK HEROES. WHO WOULD COME TO BE LITERALLY DEFINED BY HERA.
HERACLES. "THE GLORY OF HERA."
HE WAS, PERHAPS, THE MOST LIKE HIS FATHER OF ALL ZEUS'S CHILDREN: DIVINE, MORTAL, AND ALL POINTS IN-BETWEEN.
PERHAPS THAT IS WHY HERA DETESTED HIM SO.
THERE IS A STORY THEY TELL OF HERACLES.
WHETHER OR NOT IT IS TRUE IS UNIMPORTANT.
ONE DAY, HERACLES CAME TO A FORK IN THE ROAD. IN EACH OF THE PATHS STOOD A WOMAN.

ONE PATH WAS STEEP AND ROCKY, AND OVERGROWN WITH THORNS AND THISTLES. THE WOMAN WHO STOOD UPON IT WAS DRESSED SOMBERLY, HER FACE HIDDEN IN SHADOW.

SHE SPOKE TO HERACLES. "TAKE MY PATH," SHE SAID, "FOR THOUGH IT IS LONG, AND HARD, AT THE END YOU SHALL BE REWARDED, YOUR HARD WORK AND TOIL RECOGNIZED. YOU WILL BE REMEMBERED FOREVER."

THE OTHER PATH SLOPED GENTLY DOWNWARD. FRUIT TREES PROVIDED COOL SHADE, AND A GENTLE BREEZE CARRIED THE SMELL OF FLOWERS TO HERACLES' NOSE. THE WOMAN WHO STOOD UPON IT WAS BEAUTIFUL, AND DRESSED IN LIGHT, GAUZY ROBES.

"WHY BOTHER WITH ALL THAT TROUBLE," SHE CALLED TO HERACLES. "ONE SUCH AS YOU SHOULD NOT HAVE TO TOIL AND SWEAT. TAKE MY PATH, AND ALL YOU DESIRE WILL BE GIVEN TO YOU."

FOR A LONG TIME, HERACLES STOOD BEFORE THE TWO WOMEN.

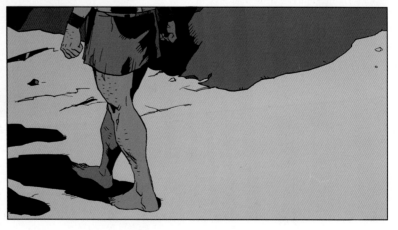

HERACLES' HARD ROAD BEGAN EVEN BEFORE HE WAS BORN. HIS MOTHER, ALCMENE, WAS THE GRANDDAUGHTER OF PERSEUS AND ANDROMEDA, WHOSE CHILDREN HAD GONE ON TO FOUND MANY OF THE GREATEST CITIES OF GREECE.

THEIRS WAS THE MIGHTIEST ROYAL FAMILY IN ANTIQUITY. AND ZEUS WANTED A CHILD OF HIS TO BE THEIR HEAD. HE PRONOUNCED TO THE GODS ON OLYMPUS:

THE NEXT-BORN CHILD OF THE LINE OF PERSEUS AND ANDROMEDA SHALL BE KING OF ALL MYCENAE.

ONE DAY, TO ENSURE THAT THE CHILD WOULD BE HIS, ZEUS VISITED ALCMENE IN THE BODY OF HER HUSBAND, AMPHITRYON.

SOON ALCMENE WAS HEAVY WITH CHILD. ZEUS'S PLAN SEEMED TO HAVE WORKED.

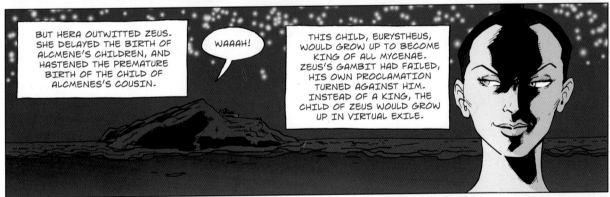

BUT HERA OUTWITTED ZEUS. SHE DELAYED THE BIRTH OF ALCMENE'S CHILDREN, AND HASTENED THE PREMATURE BIRTH OF THE CHILD OF ALCMENES'S COUSIN.

WAAAH!

THIS CHILD, EURYSTHEUS, WOULD GROW UP TO BECOME KING OF ALL MYCENAE. ZEUS'S GAMBIT HAD FAILED, HIS OWN PROCLAMATION TURNED AGAINST HIM. INSTEAD OF A KING, THE CHILD OF ZEUS WOULD GROW UP IN VIRTUAL EXILE.

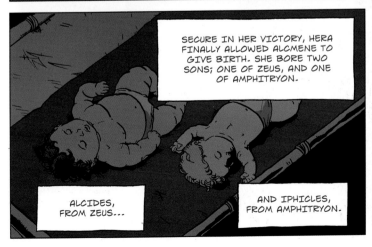

SECURE IN HER VICTORY, HERA FINALLY ALLOWED ALCMENE TO GIVE BIRTH. SHE BORE TWO SONS; ONE OF ZEUS, AND ONE OF AMPHITRYON.

ALCIDES, FROM ZEUS...

AND IPHICLES, FROM AMPHITRYON.

BUT STILL HERA WAS NOT FINISHED WITH THE BABE WHO WOULD BE HERACLES.

23

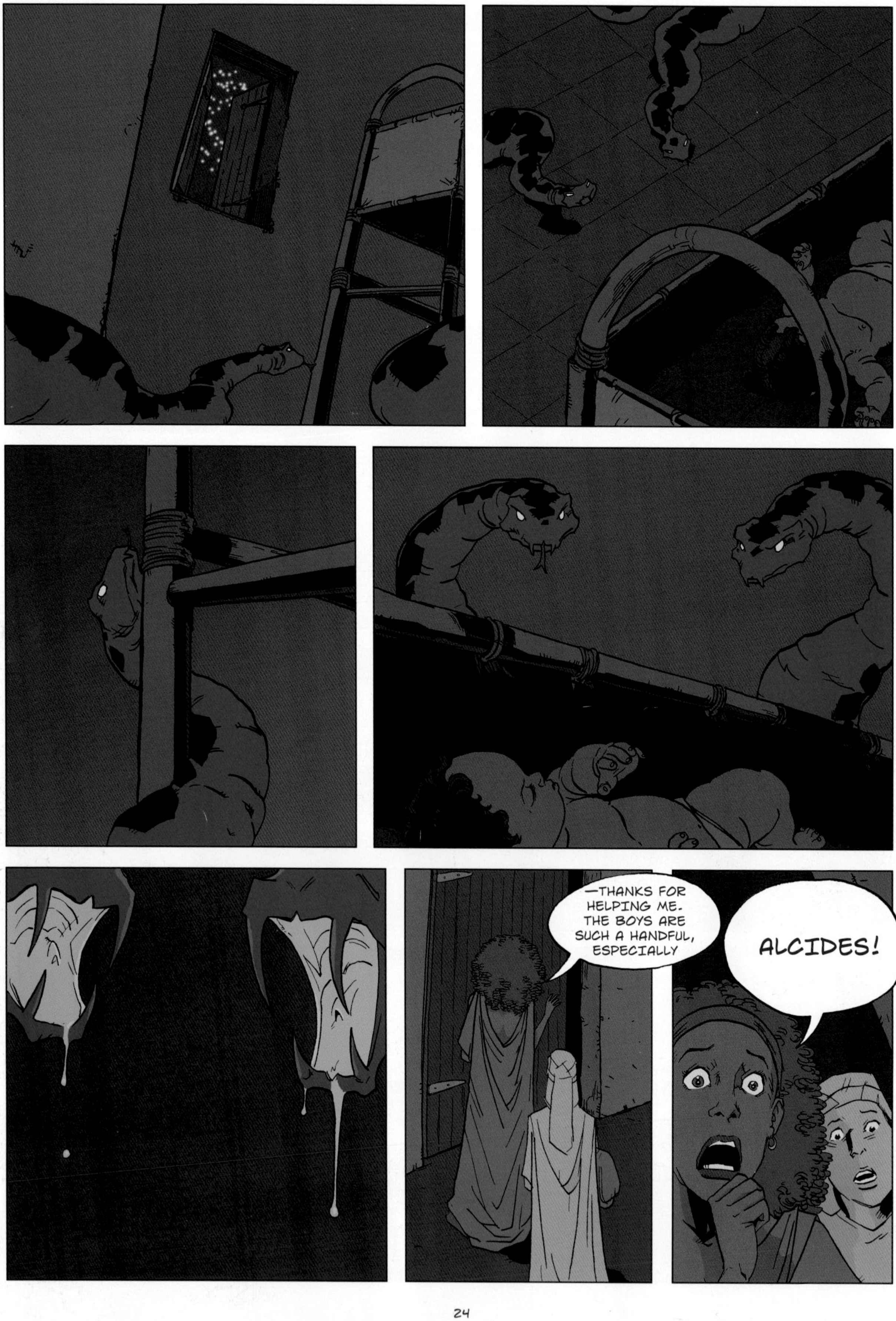
—THANKS FOR HELPING ME. THE BOYS ARE SUCH A HANDFUL, ESPECIALLY
ALCIDES!

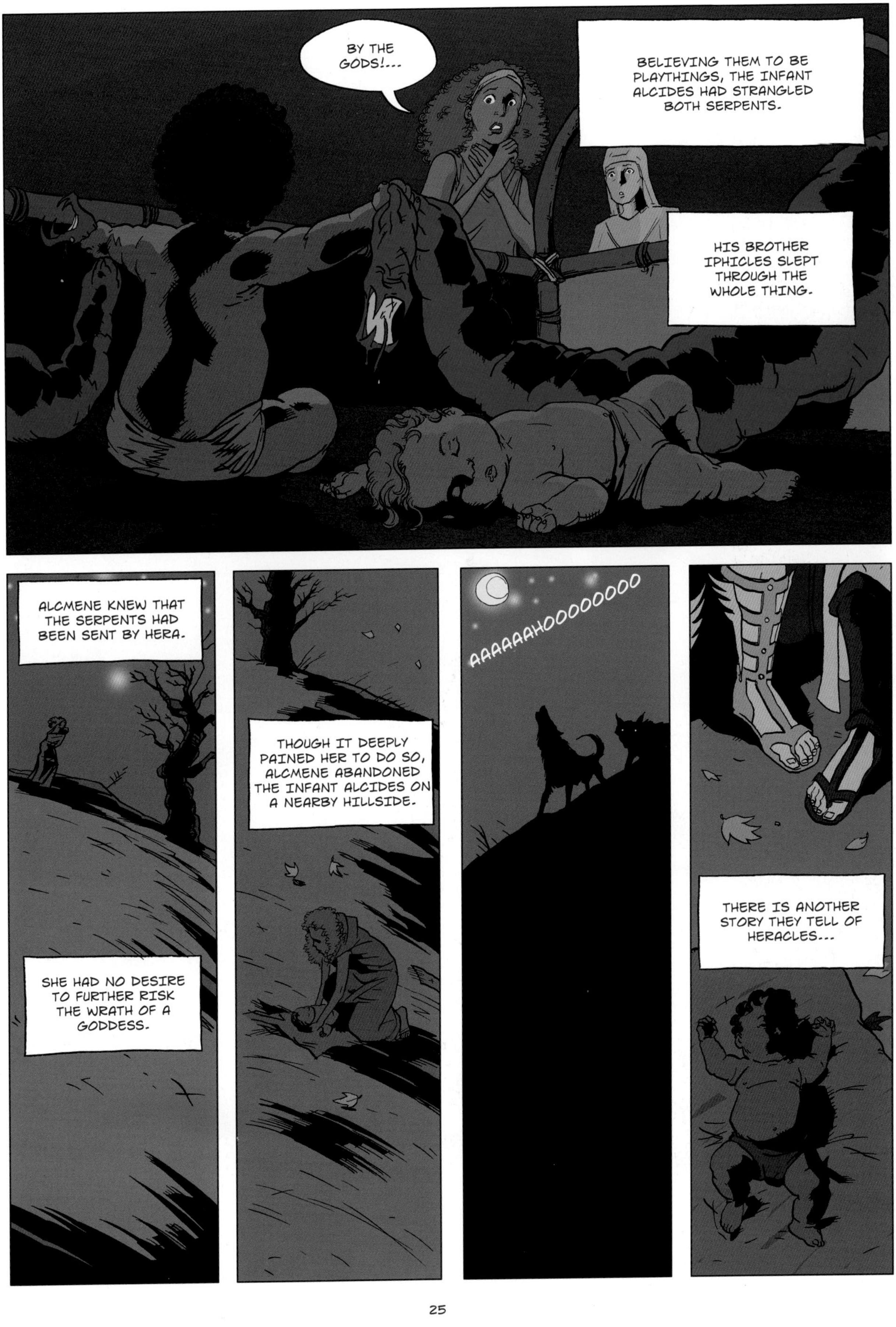
BY THE GODS!...
BELIEVING THEM TO BE PLAYTHINGS, THE INFANT ALCIDES HAD STRANGLED BOTH SERPENTS.
HIS BROTHER IPHICLES SLEPT THROUGH THE WHOLE THING.
ALCMENE KNEW THAT THE SERPENTS HAD BEEN SENT BY HERA.
SHE HAD NO DESIRE TO FURTHER RISK THE WRATH OF A GODDESS.
THOUGH IT DEEPLY PAINED HER TO DO SO, ALCMENE ABANDONED THE INFANT ALCIDES ON A NEARBY HILLSIDE.
AAAAAAHOOOOOOOOO
THERE IS ANOTHER STORY THEY TELL OF HERACLES...

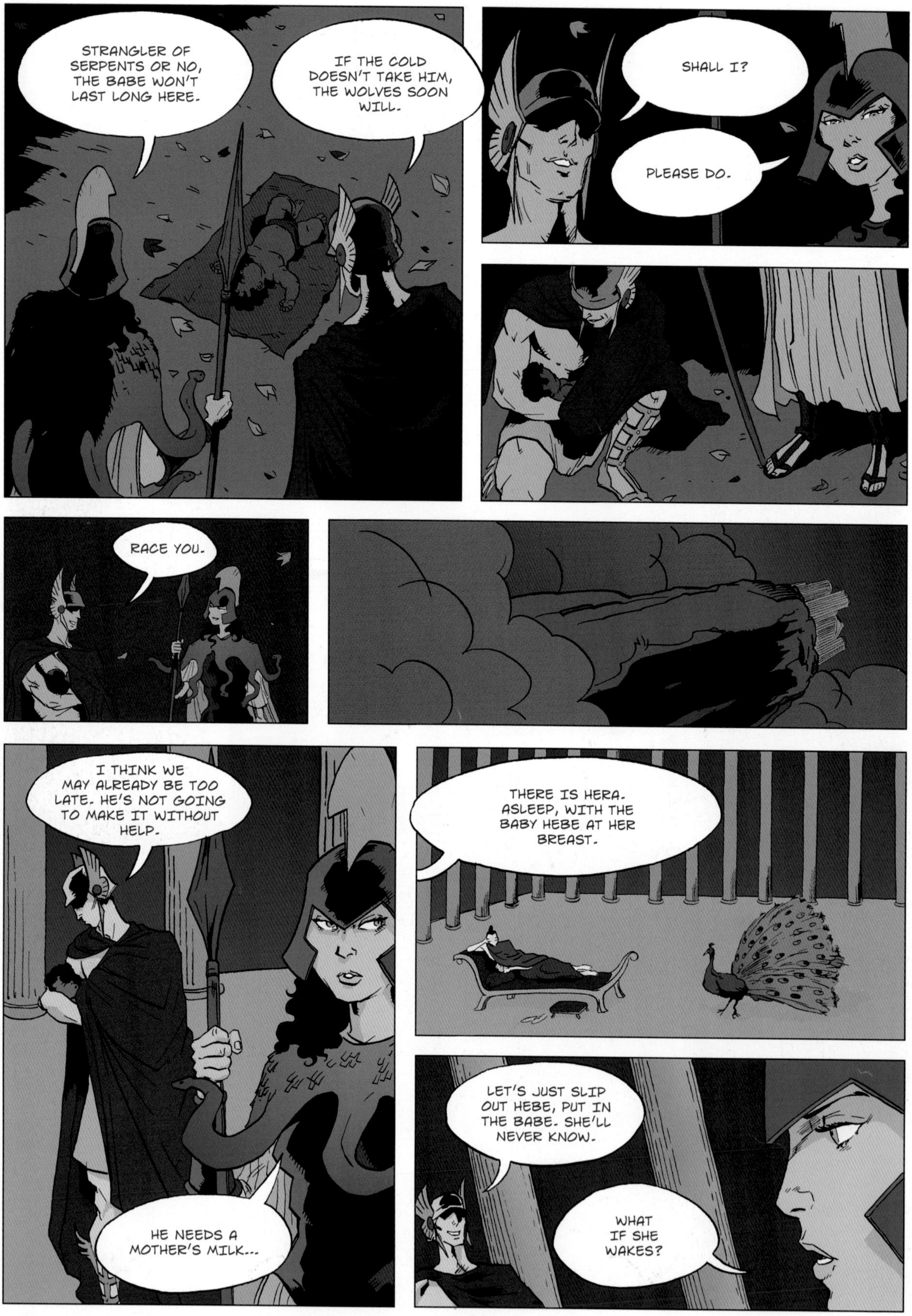

STRANGLER OF SERPENTS OR NO, THE BABE WON'T LAST LONG HERE.
IF THE COLD DOESN'T TAKE HIM, THE WOLVES SOON WILL.
SHALL I?
PLEASE DO.
RACE YOU.
I THINK WE MAY ALREADY BE TOO LATE. HE'S NOT GOING TO MAKE IT WITHOUT HELP.
HE NEEDS A MOTHER'S MILK...
THERE IS HERA. ASLEEP, WITH THE BABY HEBE AT HER BREAST.
LET'S JUST SLIP OUT HEBE, PUT IN THE BABE. SHE'LL NEVER KNOW.
WHAT IF SHE WAKES?

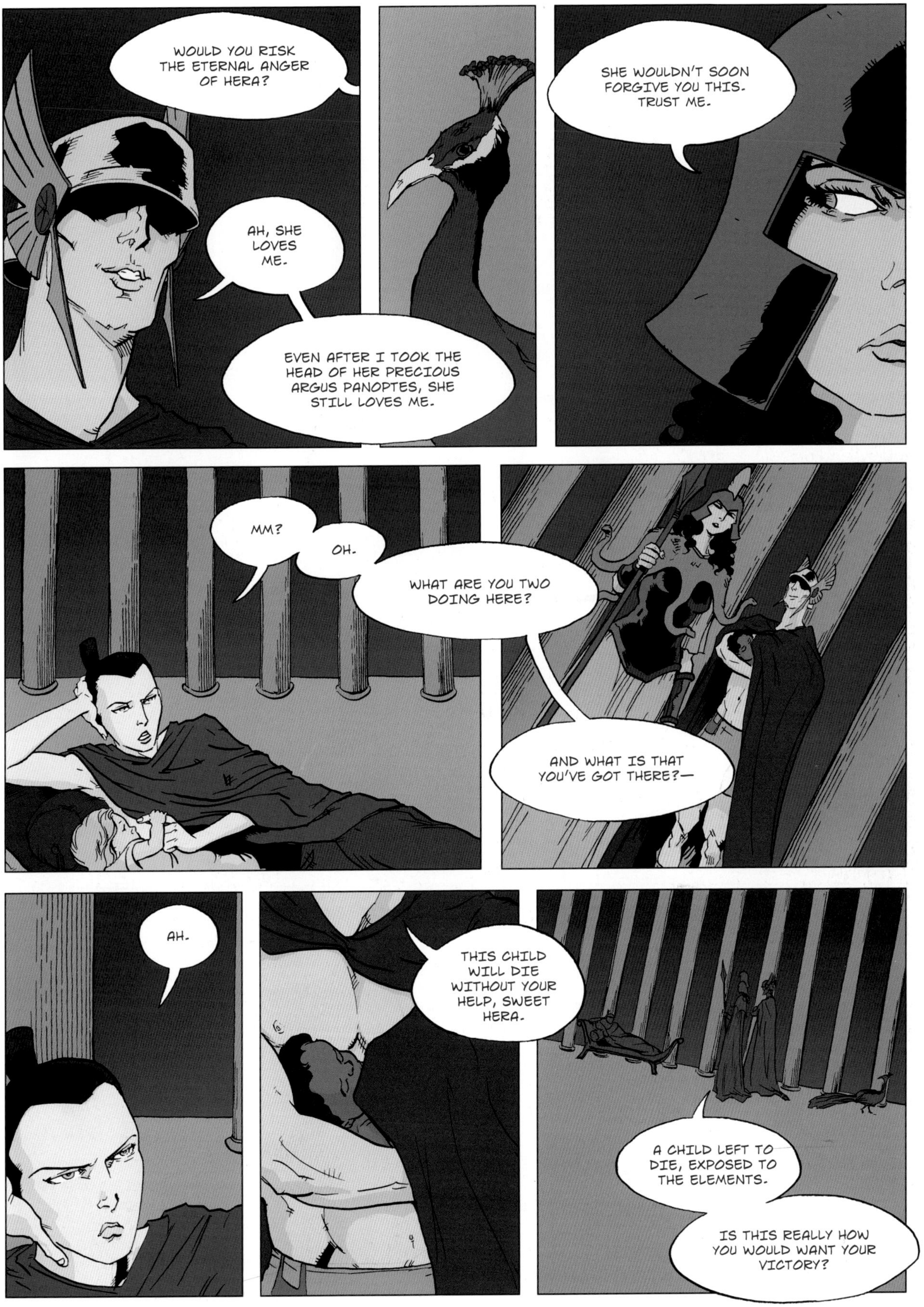
WOULD YOU RISK THE ETERNAL ANGER OF HERA?
AH, SHE LOVES ME.
EVEN AFTER I TOOK THE HEAD OF HER PRECIOUS ARGUS PANOPTES, SHE STILL LOVES ME.
SHE WOULDN'T SOON FORGIVE YOU THIS. TRUST ME.
MM?
OH.
WHAT ARE YOU TWO DOING HERE?
AND WHAT IS THAT YOU'VE GOT THERE?—
AH.
THIS CHILD WILL DIE WITHOUT YOUR HELP, SWEET HERA.
A CHILD LEFT TO DIE, EXPOSED TO THE ELEMENTS.
IS THIS REALLY HOW YOU WOULD WANT YOUR VICTORY?

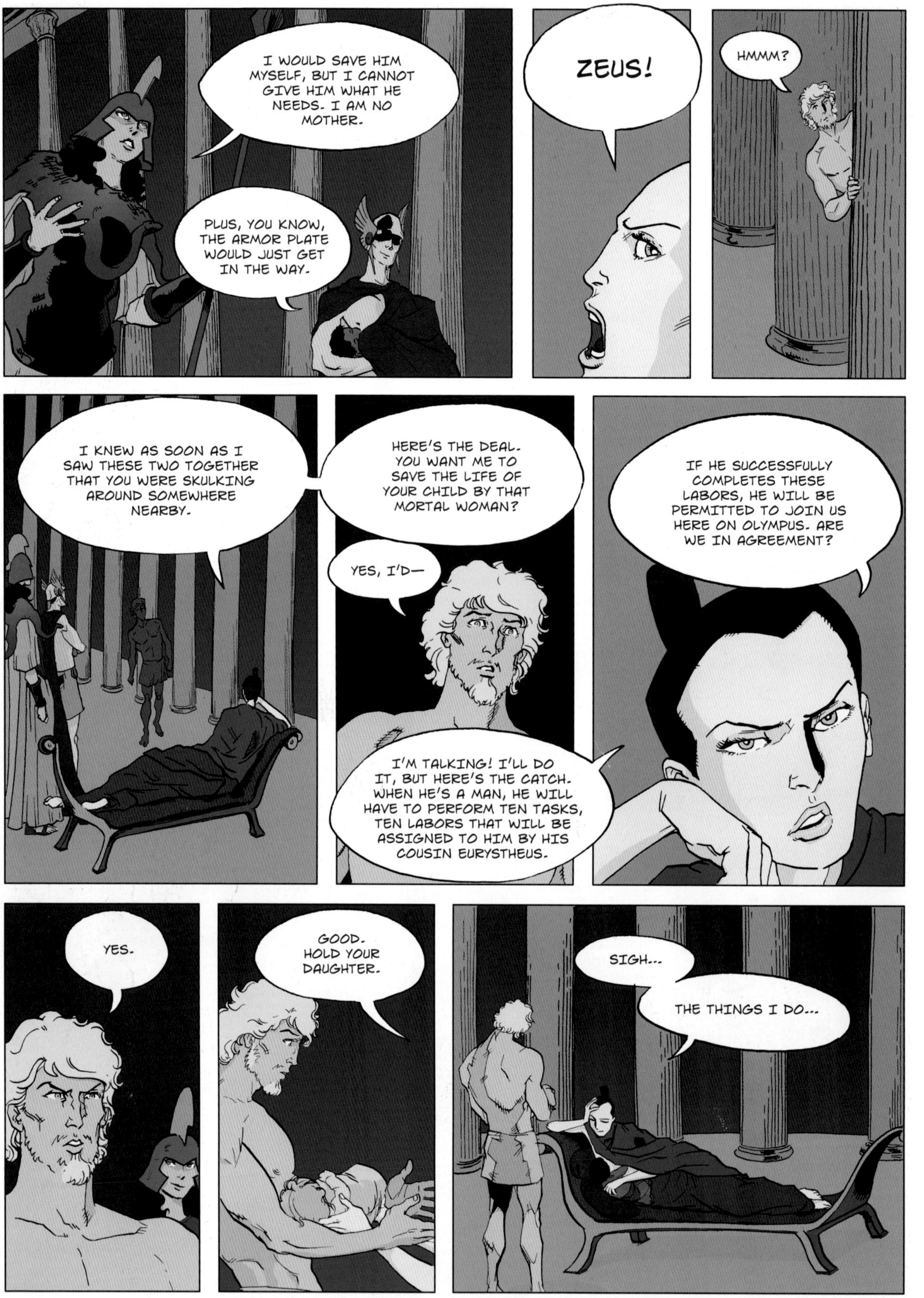
I WOULD SAVE HIM MYSELF, BUT I CANNOT GIVE HIM WHAT HE NEEDS. I AM NO MOTHER.
PLUS, YOU KNOW, THE ARMOR PLATE WOULD JUST GET IN THE WAY.
ZEUS!
HMMM?
I KNEW AS SOON AS I SAW THESE TWO TOGETHER THAT YOU WERE SKULKING AROUND SOMEWHERE NEARBY.
HERE'S THE DEAL. YOU WANT ME TO SAVE THE LIFE OF YOUR CHILD BY THAT MORTAL WOMAN?
YES, I'D—
I'M TALKING! I'LL DO IT, BUT HERE'S THE CATCH. WHEN HE'S A MAN, HE WILL HAVE TO PERFORM TEN TASKS, TEN LABORS THAT WILL BE ASSIGNED TO HIM BY HIS COUSIN EURYSTHEUS.
IF HE SUCCESSFULLY COMPLETES THESE LABORS, HE WILL BE PERMITTED TO JOIN US HERE ON OLYMPUS. ARE WE IN AGREEMENT?
YES.
GOOD. HOLD YOUR DAUGHTER.
SIGH...
THE THINGS I DO...

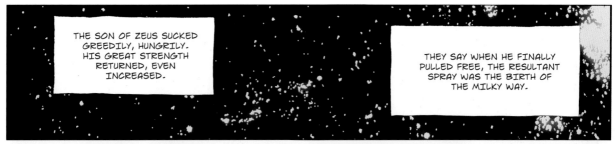

THE SON OF ZEUS SUCKED GREEDILY, HUNGRILY. HIS GREAT STRENGTH RETURNED, EVEN INCREASED.

THEY SAY WHEN HE FINALLY PULLED FREE, THE RESULTANT SPRAY WAS THE BIRTH OF THE MILKY WAY.

YEARS PASSED...

DO YOU KNOW WHY YOU HAVE COME TO ME?

THE ORACLE AT DELPHI INSTRUCTED ME TO DO SO.

OH YES, APOLLO'S ORACLE.

THOUGH, ON OCCASION OTHER GODS HAVE BEEN KNOWN TO SPEAK THROUGH IT.

THEN YOU ALSO KNOW WHAT YOU MUST DO. I WILL ASSIGN TO YOU TEN TASKS, TEN LABORS FOR THE BETTERMENT OF ALL MANKIND.

FOR I AM A WISE AND BENEVOLENT KING, AND I DO THESE THINGS TO YOU TO MAKE THE WORLD A BETTER AND SAFER PLACE.

THERE IS A LION THAT TERRORIZES THE LAND OF NEMEA. IT'S NO NORMAL BEAST. IT HAS BRAZEN CLAWS, CAPABLE OF SLICING THROUGH ANYTHING.

AND THEY SAY ITS SKIN CANNOT BE PIERCED—TO BE SURE, NO HUNTER HAS MANAGED YET TO BRING IT DOWN.

I WANT YOU TO KILL THIS NEMEAN LION.

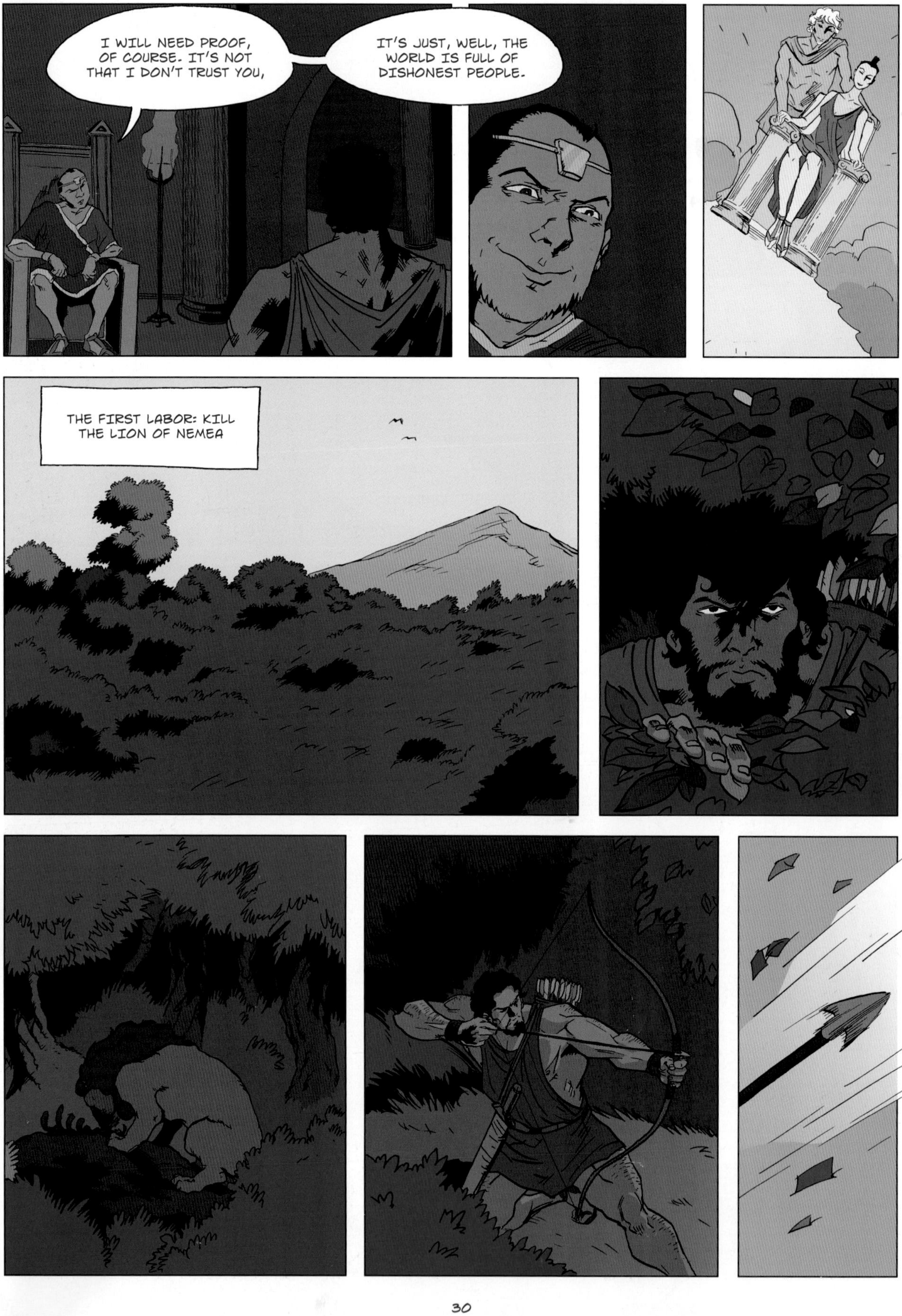
I WILL NEED PROOF, OF COURSE. IT'S NOT THAT I DON'T TRUST YOU,
IT'S JUST, WELL, THE WORLD IS FULL OF DISHONEST PEOPLE.
THE FIRST LABOR: KILL THE LION OF NEMEA

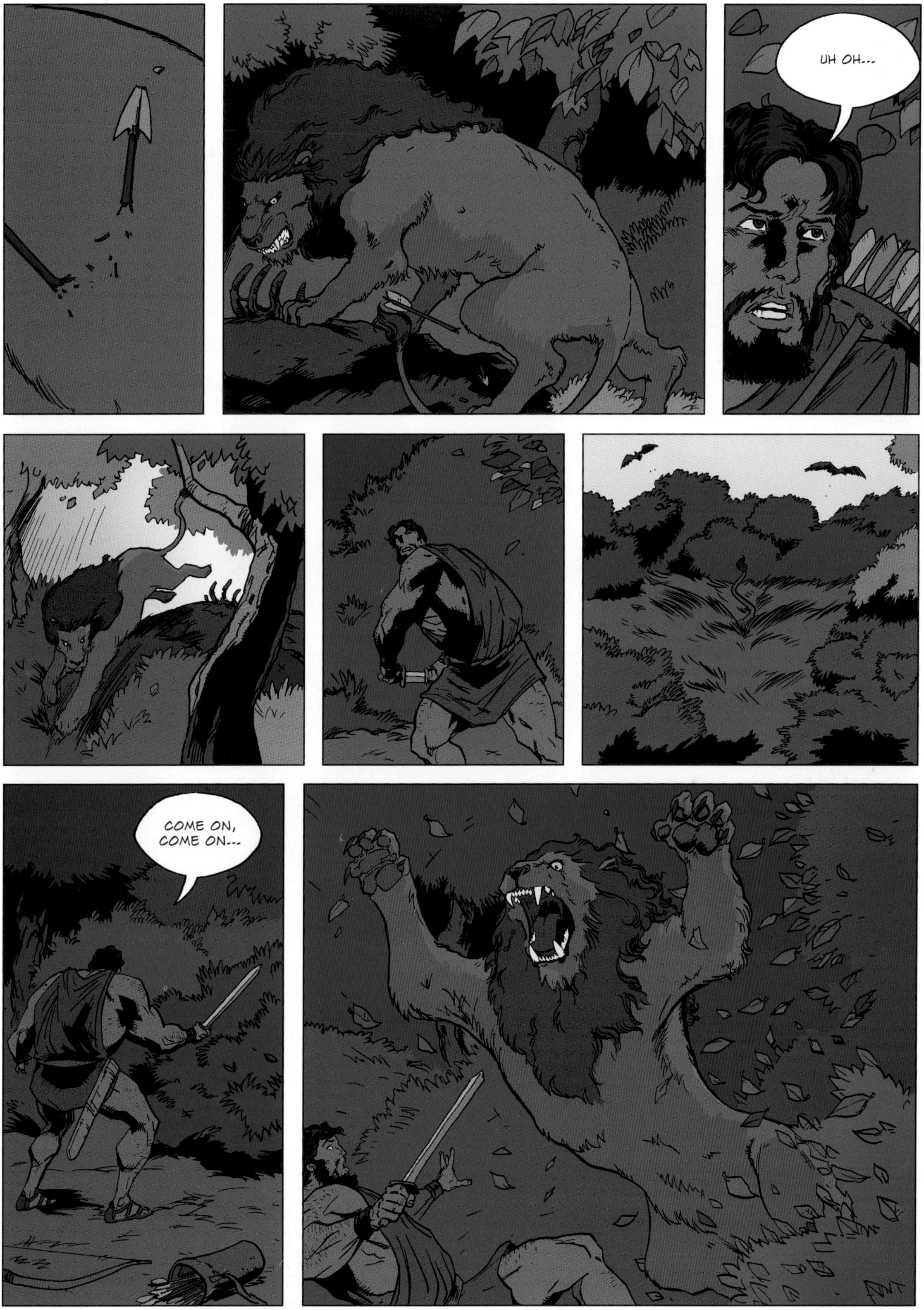
UH OH...
COME ON,
COME ON...

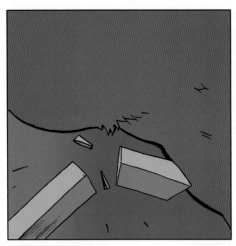

OH, FOR...

USELESS...

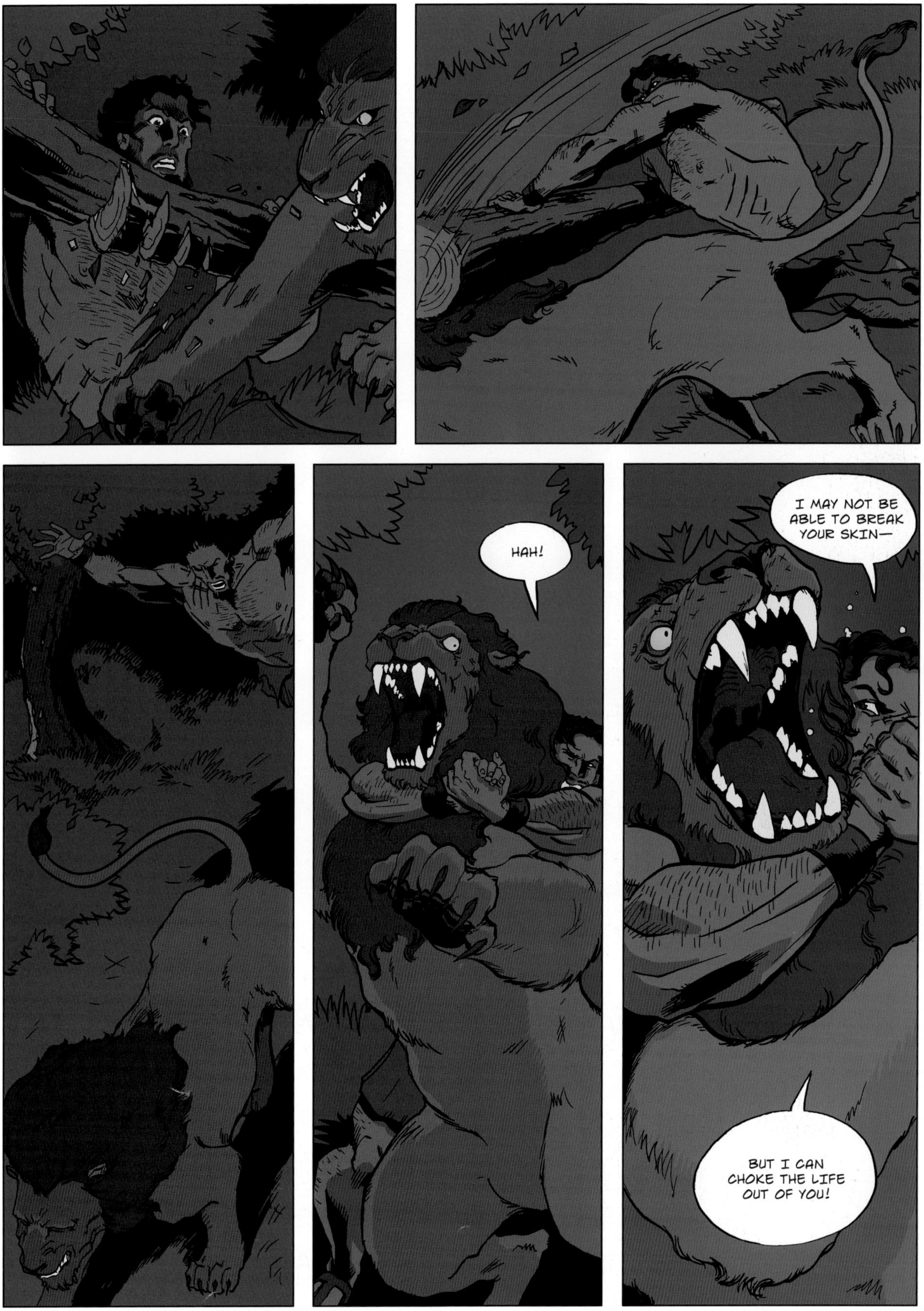
HAH!
I MAY NOT BE ABLE TO BREAK YOUR SKIN—
BUT I CAN CHOKE THE LIFE OUT OF YOU!

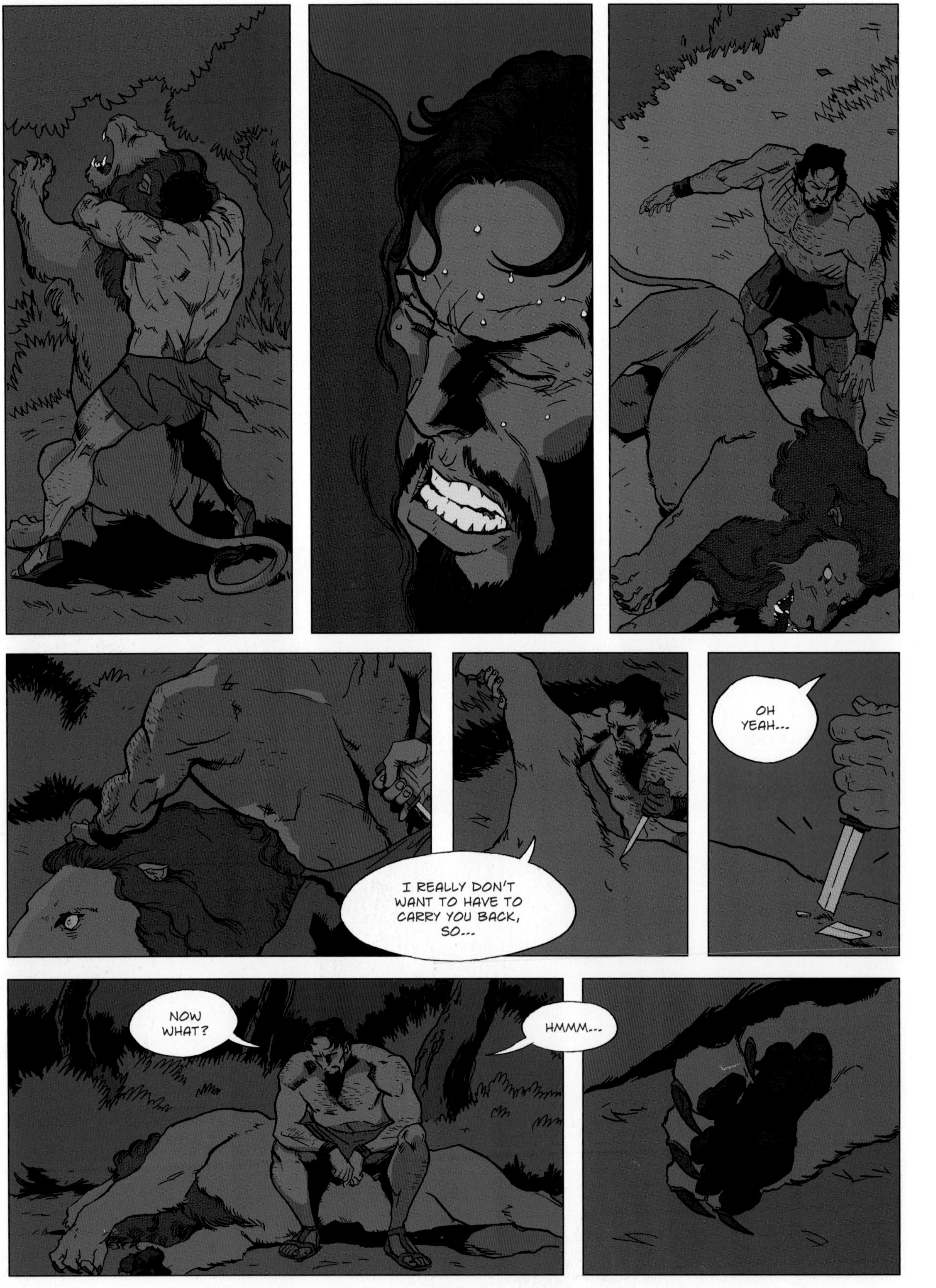
I REALLY DON'T WANT TO HAVE TO CARRY YOU BACK, SO...
OH YEAH...
NOW WHAT?
HMMM...

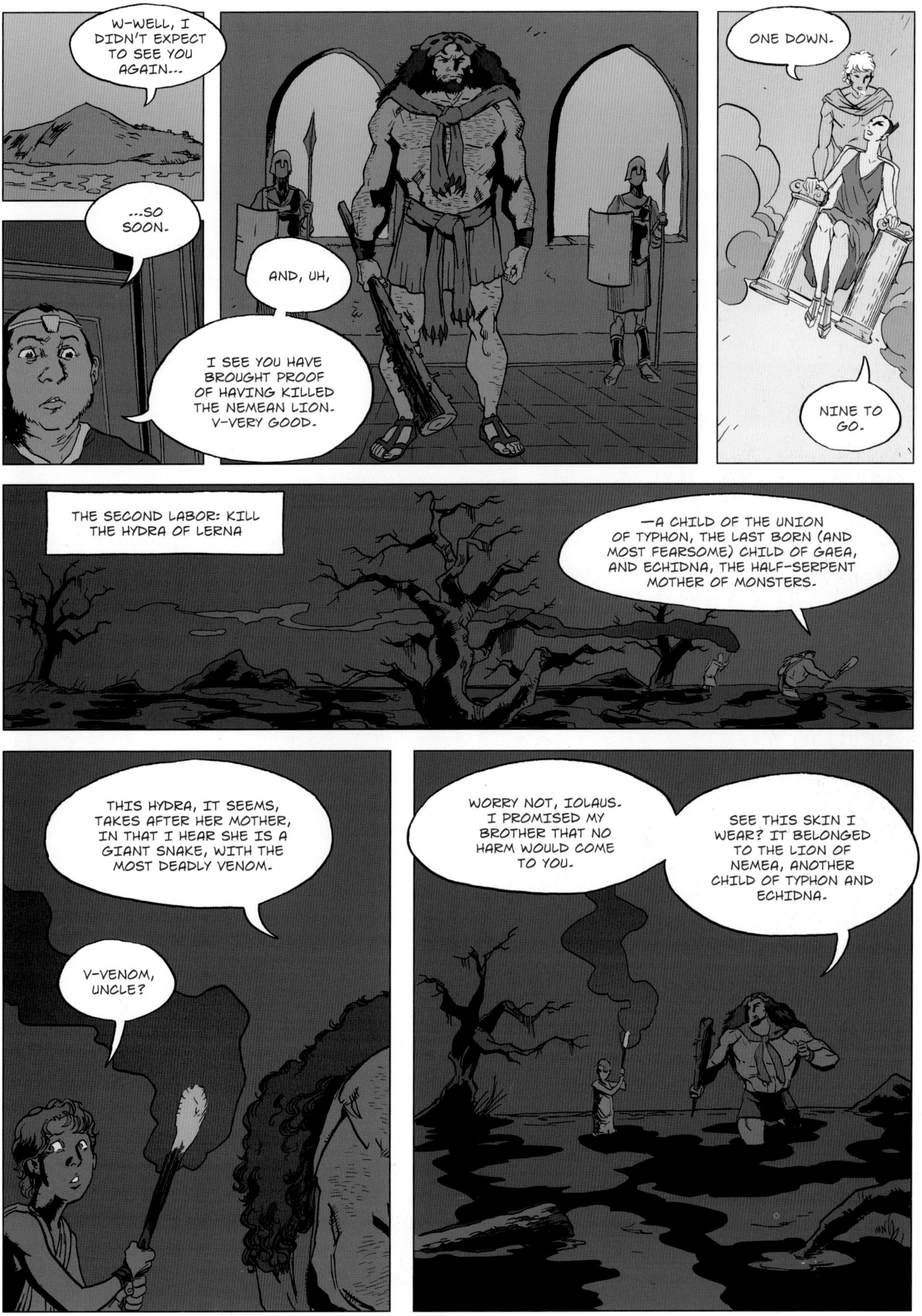
W-WELL, I DIDN'T EXPECT TO SEE YOU AGAIN...
...SO SOON.
AND, UH,
I SEE YOU HAVE BROUGHT PROOF OF HAVING KILLED THE NEMEAN LION. V-VERY GOOD.
ONE DOWN.
NINE TO GO.
THE SECOND LABOR: KILL THE HYDRA OF LERNA
—A CHILD OF THE UNION OF TYPHON, THE LAST BORN (AND MOST FEARSOME) CHILD OF GAEA, AND ECHIDNA, THE HALF-SERPENT MOTHER OF MONSTERS.
THIS HYDRA, IT SEEMS, TAKES AFTER HER MOTHER, IN THAT I HEAR SHE IS A GIANT SNAKE, WITH THE MOST DEADLY VENOM.
V-VENOM, UNCLE?
WORRY NOT, IOLAUS. I PROMISED MY BROTHER THAT NO HARM WOULD COME TO YOU.
SEE THIS SKIN I WEAR? IT BELONGED TO THE LION OF NEMEA, ANOTHER CHILD OF TYPHON AND ECHIDNA.

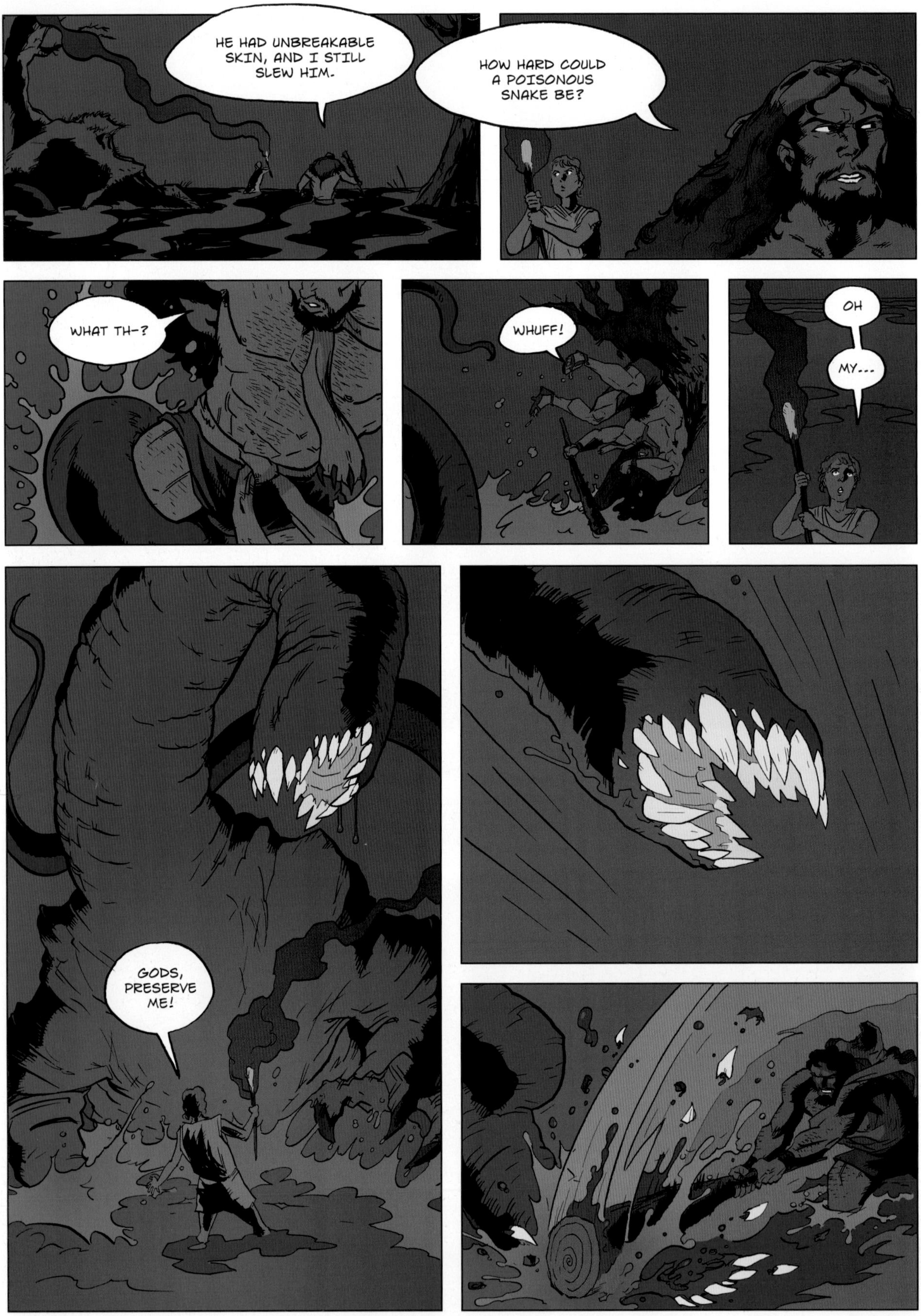
HE HAD UNBREAKABLE SKIN, AND I STILL SLEW HIM.
HOW HARD COULD A POISONOUS SNAKE BE?
WHAT TH-?
WHUFF!
OH
MY...
GODS, PRESERVE ME!

THAT'S TWO.
WAIT FOR IT...
SEE, MY NEPHEW, WHAT DID I TELL—
...YOU.
UH OH..
IOLAUS, LAD...
DON'T MAKE ME A LIAR TO YOUR FATHER—
THAT'S TWO!
AND FOUR...
AND SIX!
RUN!

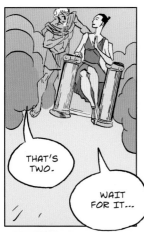

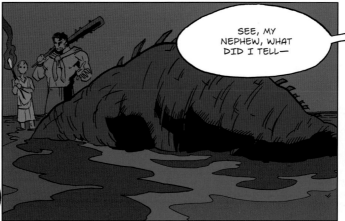

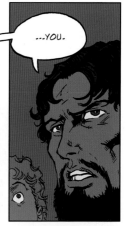

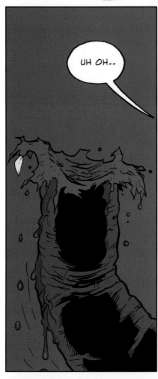

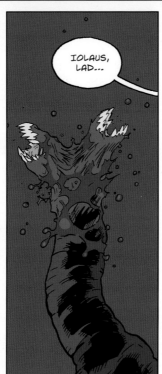

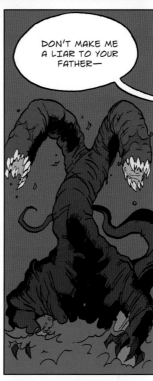

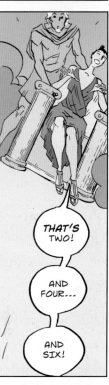

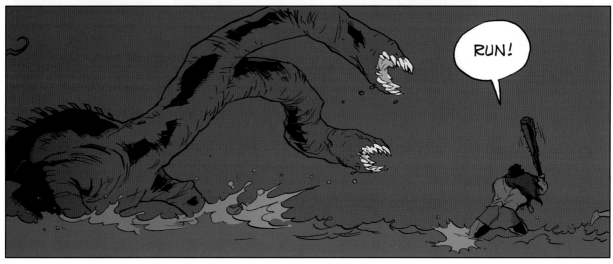

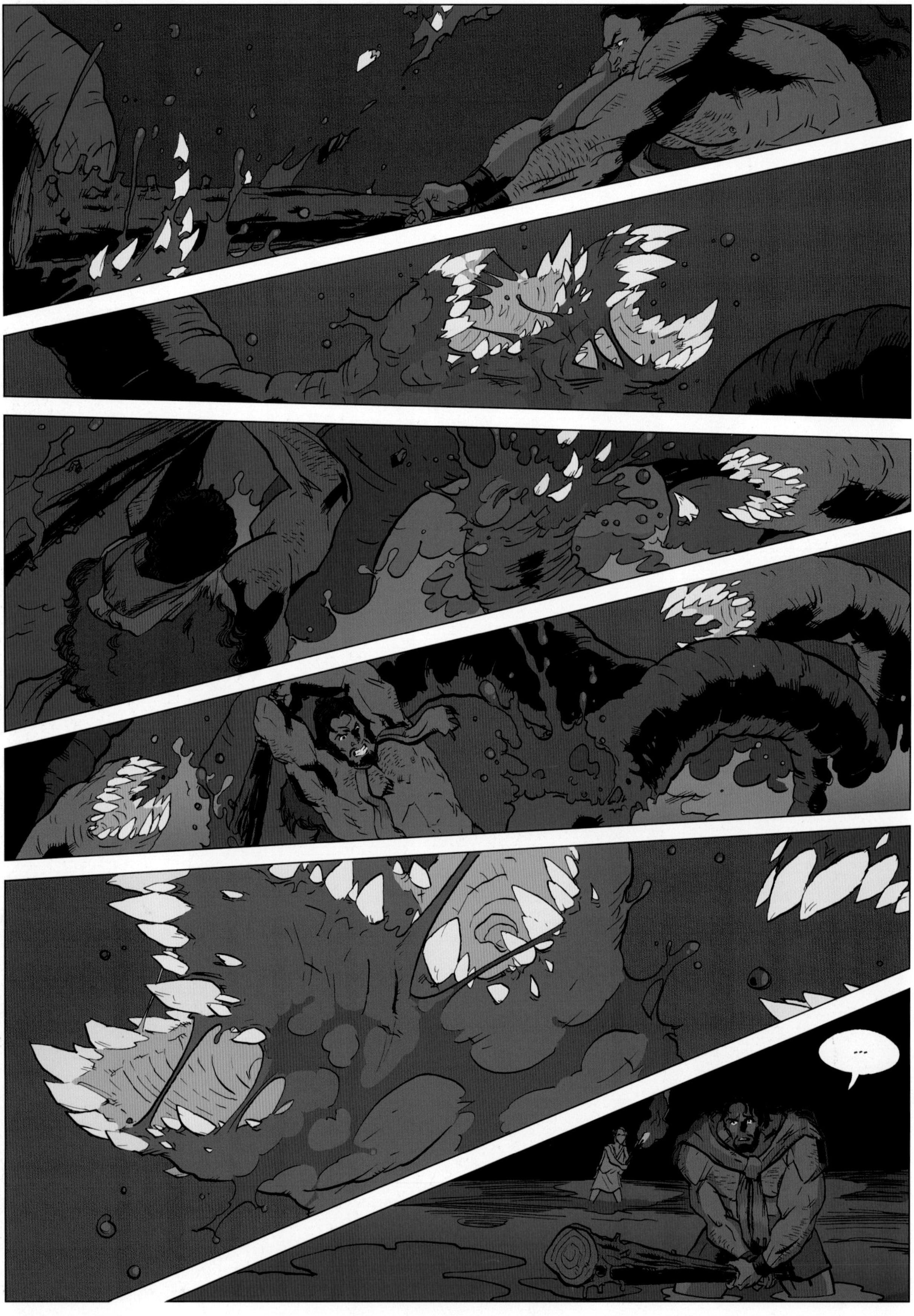
...

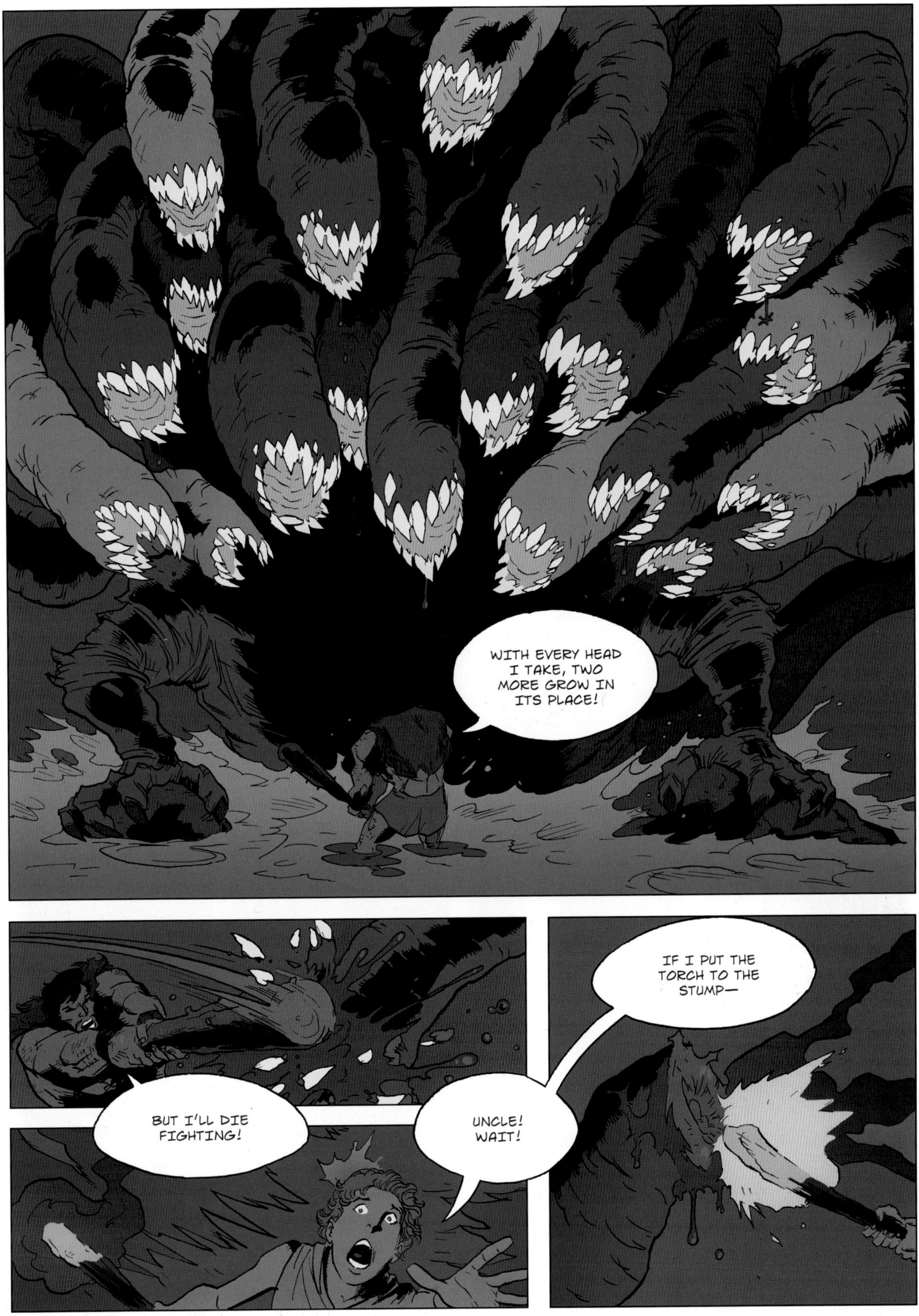
WITH EVERY HEAD I TAKE, TWO MORE GROW IN ITS PLACE!
BUT I'LL DIE FIGHTING!
UNCLE! WAIT!
IF I PUT THE TORCH TO THE STUMP—

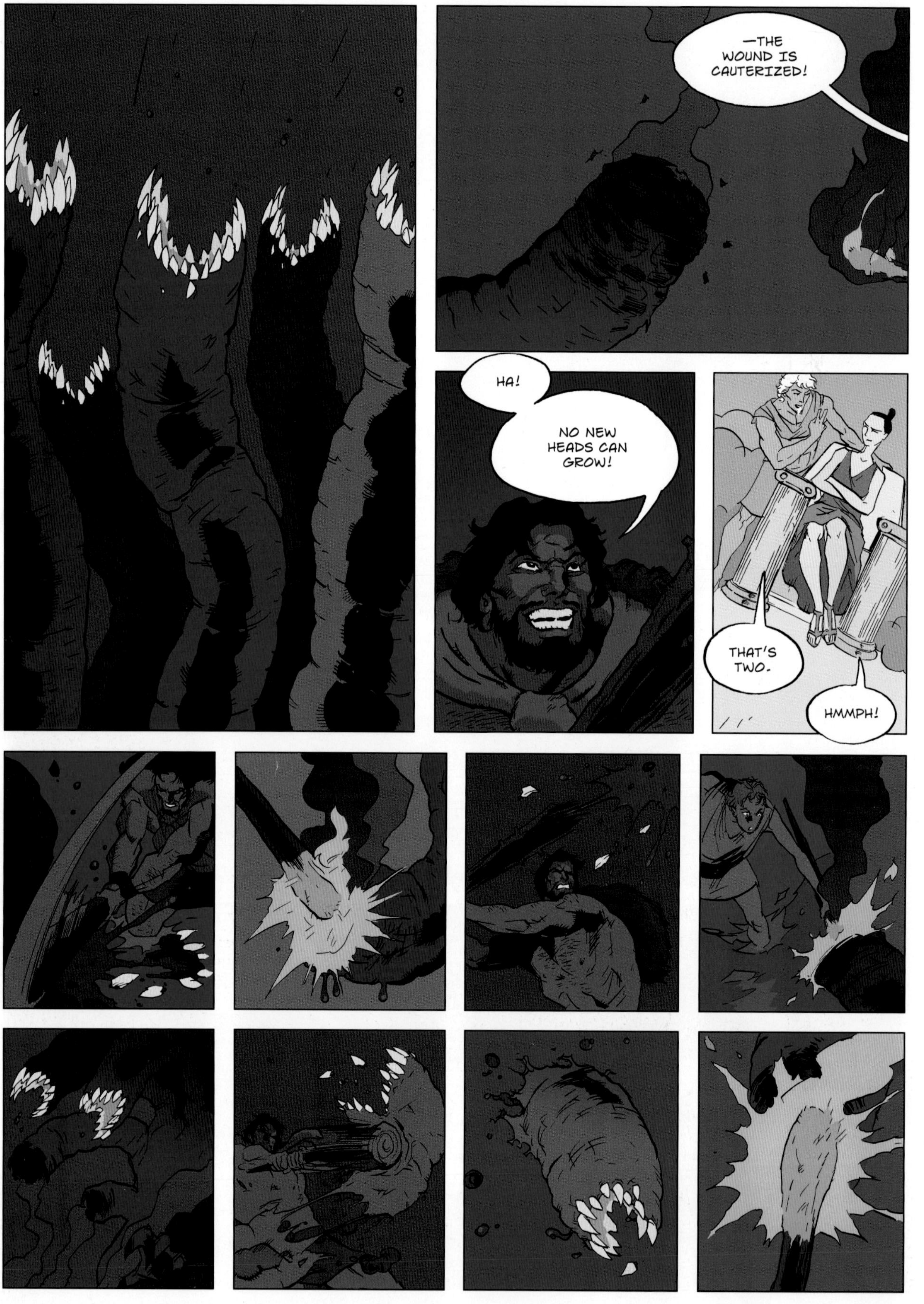
—THE WOUND IS CAUTERIZED!
HA!
NO NEW HEADS CAN GROW!
THAT'S TWO.
HMMPH!

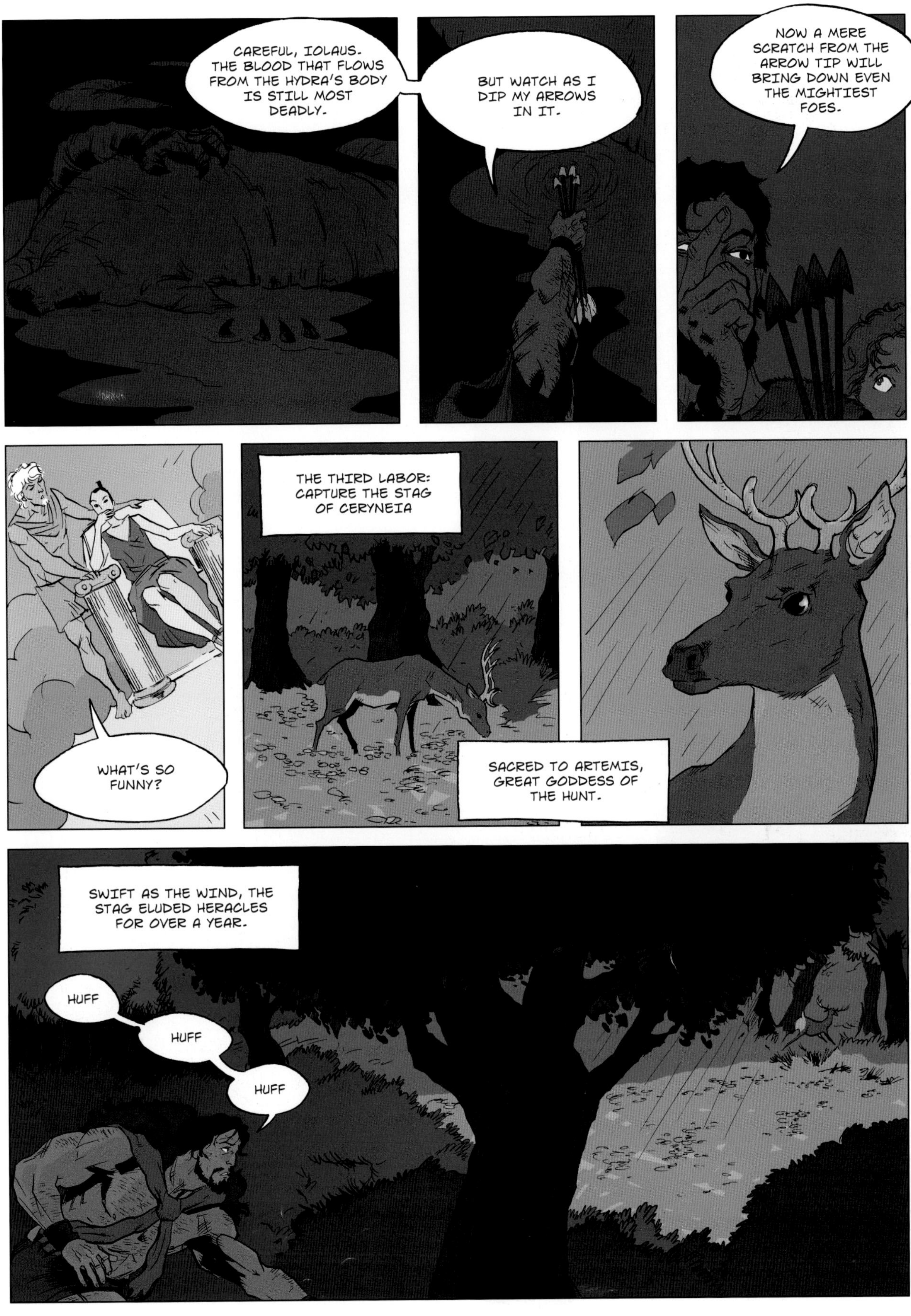
CAREFUL, IOLAUS. THE BLOOD THAT FLOWS FROM THE HYDRA'S BODY IS STILL MOST DEADLY.
BUT WATCH AS I DIP MY ARROWS IN IT.
NOW A MERE SCRATCH FROM THE ARROW TIP WILL BRING DOWN EVEN THE MIGHTIEST FOES.
WHAT'S SO FUNNY?
THE THIRD LABOR: CAPTURE THE STAG OF CERYNEIA
SACRED TO ARTEMIS, GREAT GODDESS OF THE HUNT.
SWIFT AS THE WIND, THE STAG ELUDED HERACLES FOR OVER A YEAR.
HUFF
HUFF
HUFF

UNTIL, FINALLY...

CALM YOURSELF, DAUGHTER, THE STAG STILL LIVES. HE DIDN'T USE A POISONED ARROW...

THE FOURTH LABOR: CAPTURE THE EURYMANTHIAN BOAR

A BEAST OF MONSTROUS SIZE AND STRENGTH, IT HAD LATELY DESCENDED THE SLOPES OF MOUNT EURYMANTHUS, WHERE IT HAD TAKEN TO RAIDING THE LOCAL FARMS.

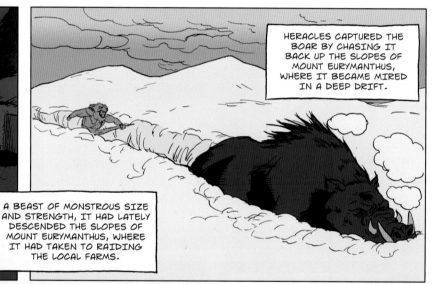

HERACLES CAPTURED THE BOAR BY CHASING IT BACK UP THE SLOPES OF MOUNT EURYMANTHUS, WHERE IT BECAME MIRED IN A DEEP DRIFT.

THE FIFTH LABOR: DESTROY THE STYMPHALIAN BIRDS

A FLOCK OF MAN-EATING BIRDS, WHOSE RAZOR-SHARP METAL FEATHERS COULD BE FIRED LIKE ARROWS, HAD LONG LAID WASTE TO THE AREA AROUND LAKE STYMPHALOS.

HIDING BENEATH HIS IMPENETRABLE LION SKIN, HERACLES SHOT THEM DOWN WITH HIS POISONED ARROWS.

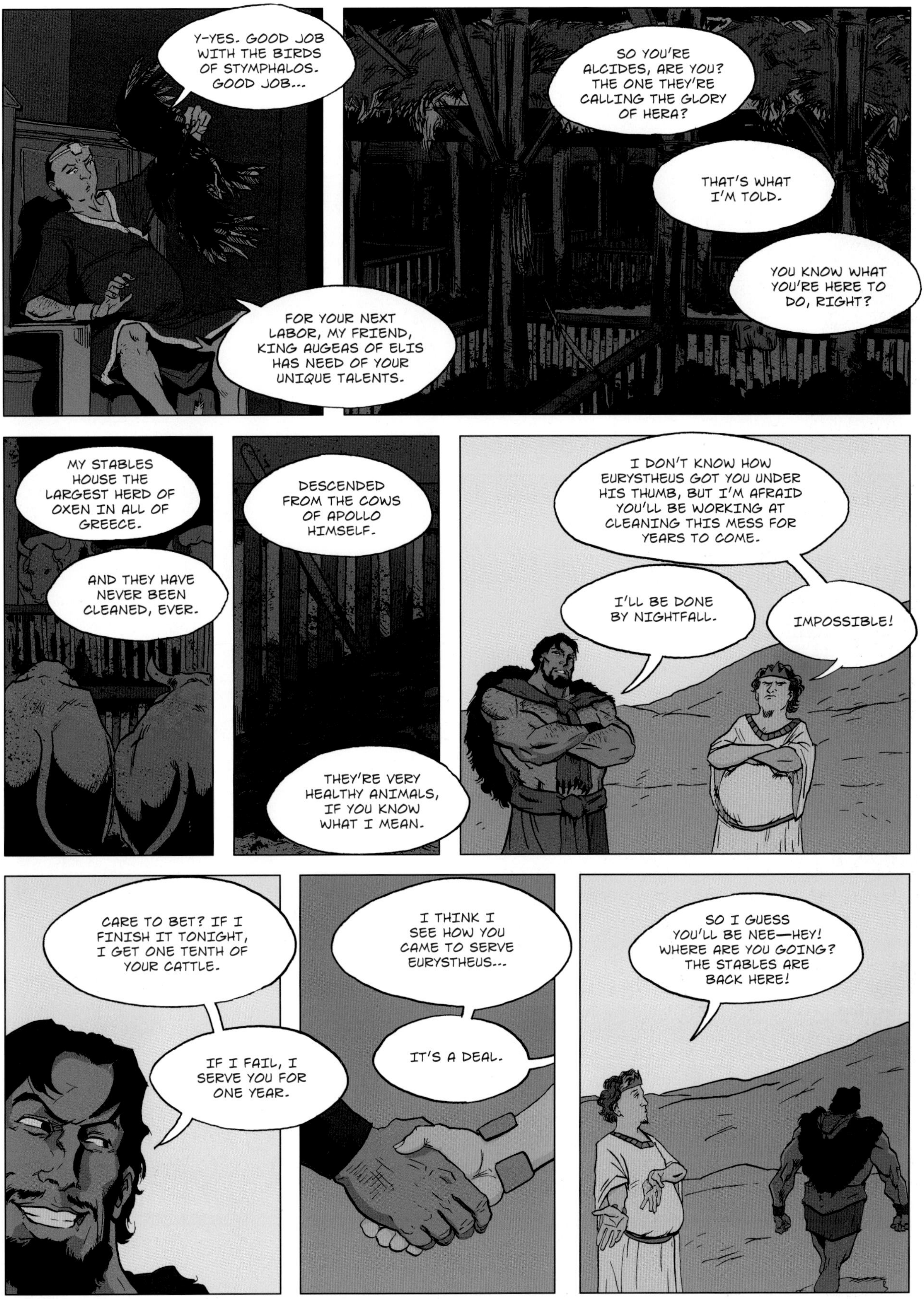
Y-YES. GOOD JOB WITH THE BIRDS OF STYMPHALOS. GOOD JOB...
FOR YOUR NEXT LABOR, MY FRIEND, KING AUGEAS OF ELIS HAS NEED OF YOUR UNIQUE TALENTS.
SO YOU'RE ALCIDES, ARE YOU? THE ONE THEY'RE CALLING THE GLORY OF HERA?
THAT'S WHAT I'M TOLD.
YOU KNOW WHAT YOU'RE HERE TO DO, RIGHT?
MY STABLES HOUSE THE LARGEST HERD OF OXEN IN ALL OF GREECE.
AND THEY HAVE NEVER BEEN CLEANED, EVER.
DESCENDED FROM THE COWS OF APOLLO HIMSELF.
THEY'RE VERY HEALTHY ANIMALS, IF YOU KNOW WHAT I MEAN.
I DON'T KNOW HOW EURYSTHEUS GOT YOU UNDER HIS THUMB, BUT I'M AFRAID YOU'LL BE WORKING AT CLEANING THIS MESS FOR YEARS TO COME.
I'LL BE DONE BY NIGHTFALL.
IMPOSSIBLE!
CARE TO BET? IF I FINISH IT TONIGHT, I GET ONE TENTH OF YOUR CATTLE.
IF I FAIL, I SERVE YOU FOR ONE YEAR.
I THINK I SEE HOW YOU CAME TO SERVE EURYSTHEUS...
IT'S A DEAL.
SO I GUESS YOU'LL BE NEE—HEY! WHERE ARE YOU GOING? THE STABLES ARE BACK HERE!

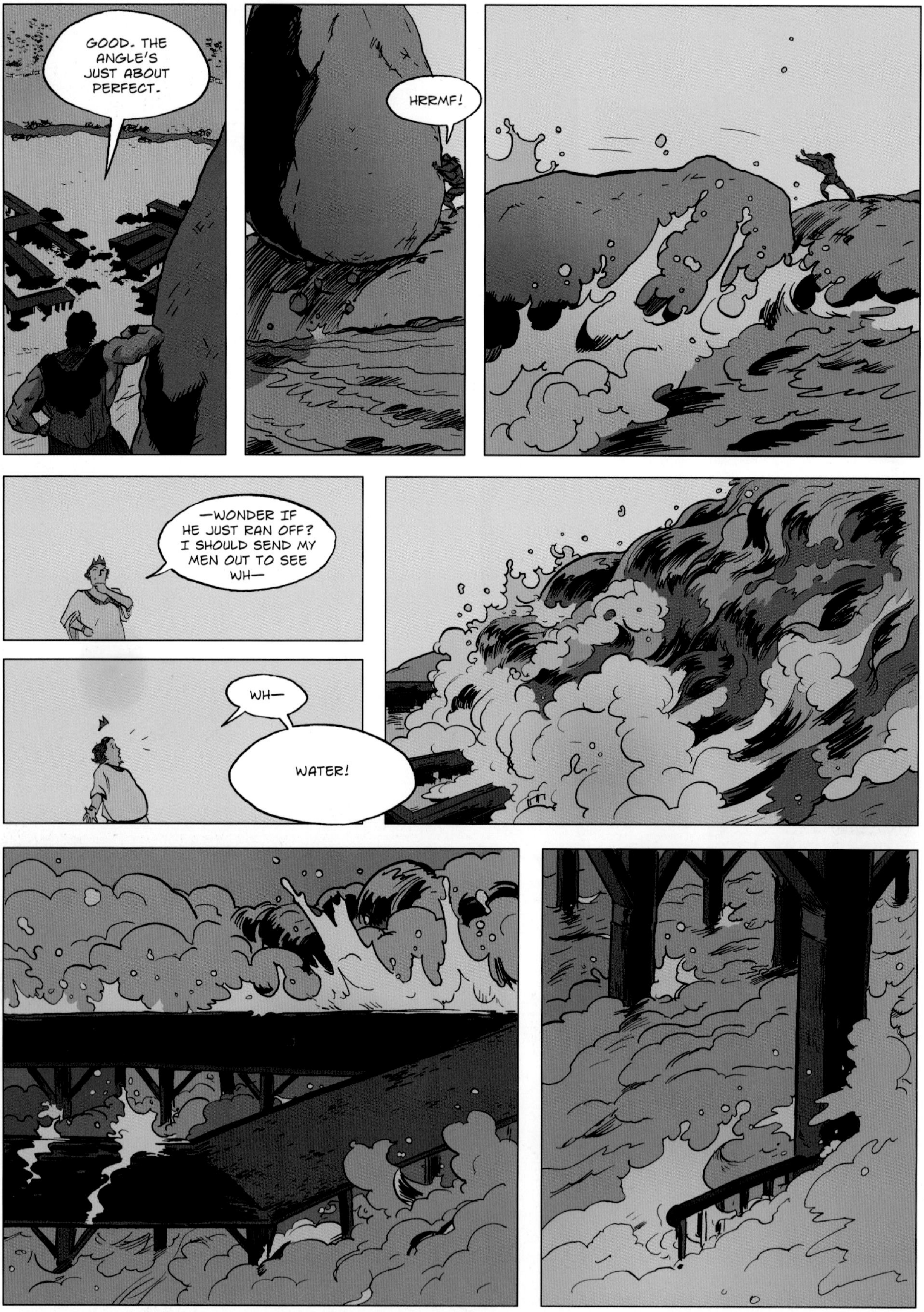
GOOD. THE ANGLE'S JUST ABOUT PERFECT.
HRRMF!
—WONDER IF HE JUST RAN OFF? I SHOULD SEND MY MEN OUT TO SEE WH—
WH—
WATER!

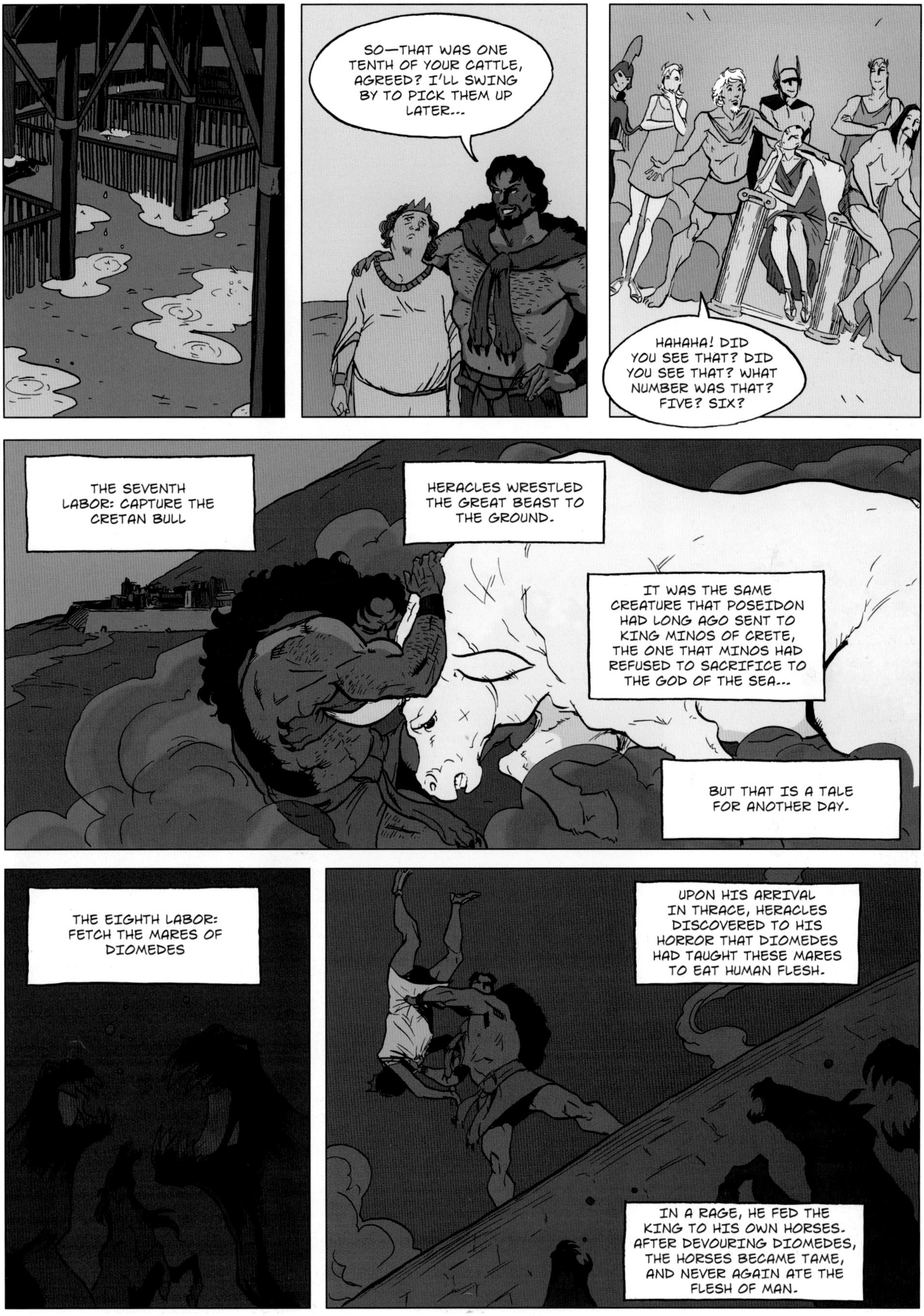
SO—THAT WAS ONE TENTH OF YOUR CATTLE, AGREED? I'LL SWING BY TO PICK THEM UP LATER...
HAHAHA! DID YOU SEE THAT? DID YOU SEE THAT? WHAT NUMBER WAS THAT? FIVE? SIX?
THE SEVENTH LABOR: CAPTURE THE CRETAN BULL
HERACLES WRESTLED THE GREAT BEAST TO THE GROUND.
IT WAS THE SAME CREATURE THAT POSEIDON HAD LONG AGO SENT TO KING MINOS OF CRETE, THE ONE THAT MINOS HAD REFUSED TO SACRIFICE TO THE GOD OF THE SEA...
BUT THAT IS A TALE FOR ANOTHER DAY.
THE EIGHTH LABOR: FETCH THE MARES OF DIOMEDES
UPON HIS ARRIVAL IN THRACE, HERACLES DISCOVERED TO HIS HORROR THAT DIOMEDES HAD TAUGHT THESE MARES TO EAT HUMAN FLESH.
IN A RAGE, HE FED THE KING TO HIS OWN HORSES. AFTER DEVOURING DIOMEDES, THE HORSES BECAME TAME, AND NEVER AGAIN ATE THE FLESH OF MAN.

THE NINTH LABOR: FETCH THE GIRDLE OF HIPPOLYTA, THE QUEEN OF THE AMAZONS AND DAUGHTER OF ARES

HOWEVER, A RUMOR AROSE THAT HERACLES MEANT TO KIDNAP THEIR QUEEN, AND HERACLES HAD TO FLEE THE WARLIKE AMAZONS, GIRDLE IN HAND.

INITIALLY, HIPPOLYTA SIMPLY AGREED TO LEND HERACLES HER GIRDLE.

JUST ONE MORE. JUST ONE MORE AND HE'S DONE IT...

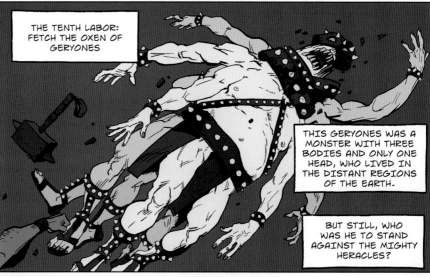

THE TENTH LABOR: FETCH THE OXEN OF GERYONES

THIS GERYONES WAS A MONSTER WITH THREE BODIES AND ONLY ONE HEAD, WHO LIVED IN THE DISTANT REGIONS OF THE EARTH.

BUT STILL, WHO WAS HE TO STAND AGAINST THE MIGHTY HERACLES?

I'M BACK.

I PRESENT TO YOU, EURYSTHEUS, THE OXEN OF GERYONES.

THAT IS IT, MY TENTH LABOR COMPLETED. MY SENTENCE TO YOU, AS SET BY THE ORACLE AT DELPHI, IS FINISHED. I AM NOW A FREE MAN.

NOT SO FAST, *HERACLES.*

YOU'RE NOT DONE WITH ME YET.

WHAT?

COME AGAIN?

THE ORACLE SAID TEN LABORS—

TO BE COMPLETED BY YOU, YES!

BUT IT WAS YOUR NEPHEW, IOLAUS, WHO FIGURED OUT HOW TO DESTROY THE HYDRA!

AND YOU ACCEPTED PAYMENT FOR THE CLEANING OF THE STABLES OF AUGEAS!

THE ORACLE APPOINTED ME THE DISPENSER OF YOUR LABORS, AND I SAY YOU STILL OWE ME...

TWO LABORS.

YOU TREACHEROUS—

THE FIRST! FETCH ME A GOLDEN APPLE FROM THE GARDEN OF THE HESPERIDES!

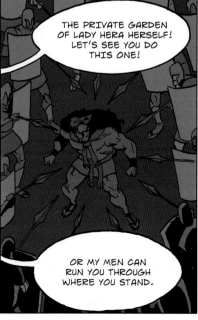

THE PRIVATE GARDEN OF LADY HERA HERSELF! LET'S SEE YOU DO THIS ONE!

OR MY MEN CAN RUN YOU THROUGH WHERE YOU STAND.

MAKE YOUR CHOICE, O "GLORY OF HERA."

AS LUCK WOULD HAVE IT, THERE WERE GAMES BEING HELD NEARBY, TO DETERMINE THE CREW OF A SHIP TO GO OUT ON ANOTHER QUEST.

ANOTHER QUEST, TO ANOTHER GARDEN. ANOTHER DRAGON GUARDING ANOTHER TREE. FOR THIS WAS ANCIENT GREECE, AND THE WORLD WAS FULL OF THESE THINGS THEN.

THESE MEN SEARCHED FOR THE GOLDEN FLEECE OF COLCHIS.

LED BY A YOUNG MAN NAMED JASON, THEY WERE TO SET OUT ON THE ARGO, THE FIRST SHIP OF ITS KIND.

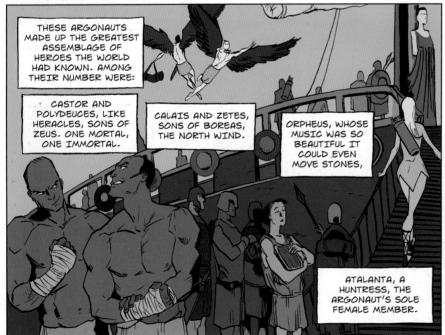

THESE ARGONAUTS MADE UP THE GREATEST ASSEMBLAGE OF HEROES THE WORLD HAD KNOWN. AMONG THEIR NUMBER WERE:

CASTOR AND POLYDEUCES, LIKE HERACLES, SONS OF ZEUS. ONE MORTAL, ONE IMMORTAL.

CALAIS AND ZETES, SONS OF BOREAS, THE NORTH WIND.

ORPHEUS, WHOSE MUSIC WAS SO BEAUTIFUL IT COULD EVEN MOVE STONES,

ATALANTA, A HUNTRESS, THE ARGONAUT'S SOLE FEMALE MEMBER.

HERACLES WAS ALREADY THE MOST FAMED HERO IN ALL OF GREECE, AND WAS WELCOMED ABOARD WITH OPEN ARMS.

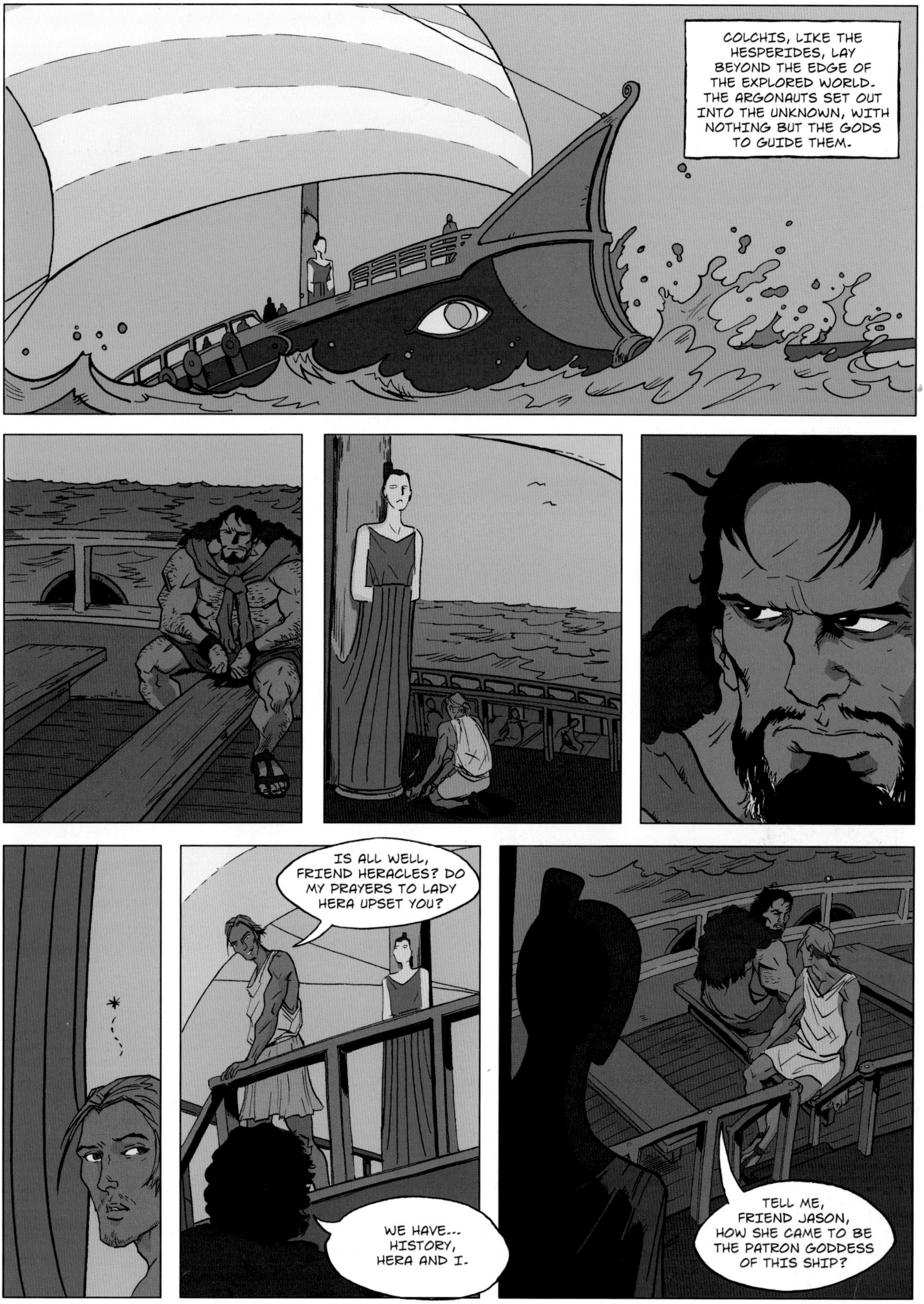
COLCHIS, LIKE THE HESPERIDES, LAY BEYOND THE EDGE OF THE EXPLORED WORLD. THE ARGONAUTS SET OUT INTO THE UNKNOWN, WITH NOTHING BUT THE GODS TO GUIDE THEM.
IS ALL WELL, FRIEND HERACLES? DO MY PRAYERS TO LADY HERA UPSET YOU?
WE HAVE... HISTORY, HERA AND I.
TELL ME, FRIEND JASON, HOW SHE CAME TO BE THE PATRON GODDESS OF THIS SHIP?

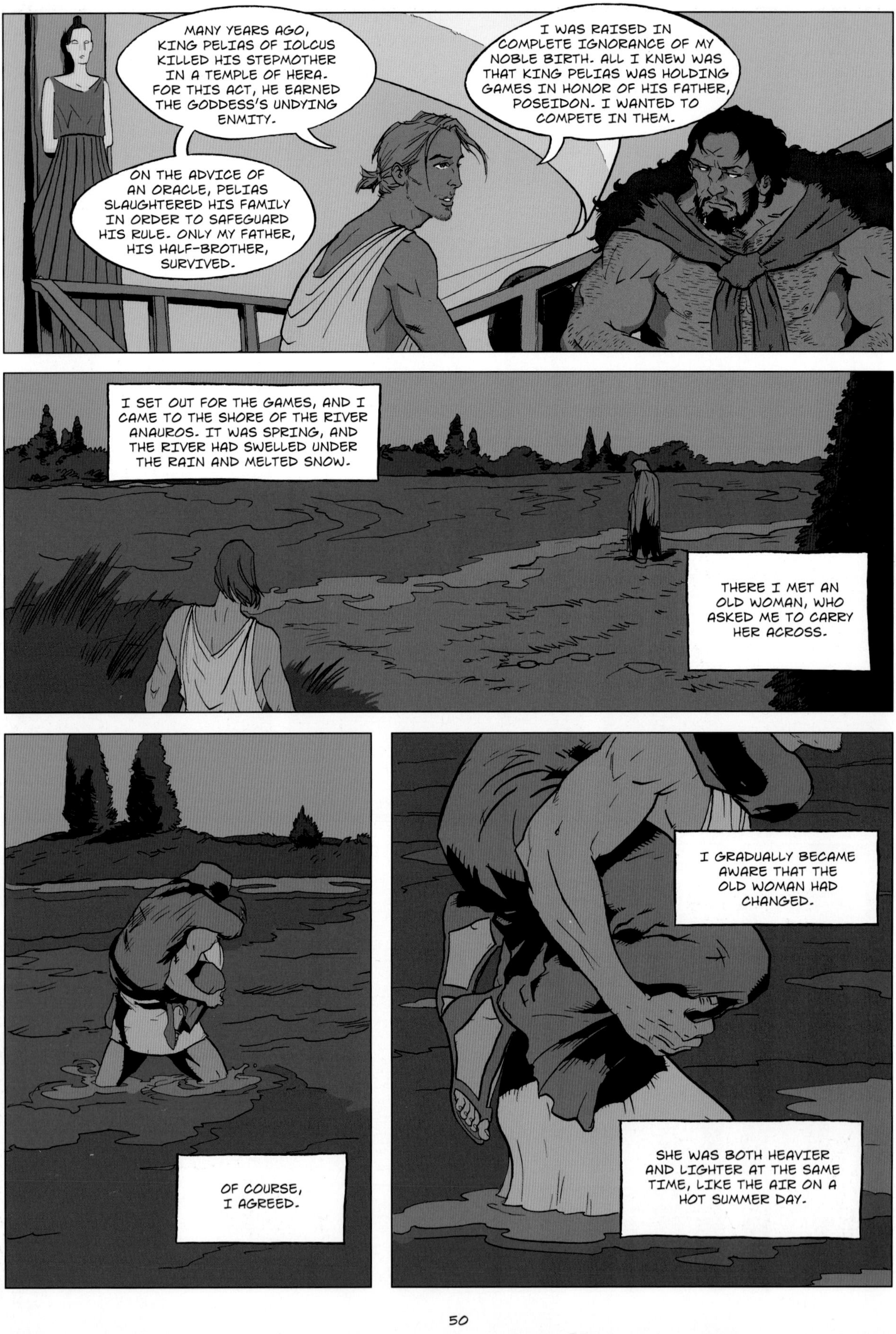
MANY YEARS AGO, KING PELIAS OF IOLCUS KILLED HIS STEPMOTHER IN A TEMPLE OF HERA. FOR THIS ACT, HE EARNED THE GODDESS'S UNDYING ENMITY.
ON THE ADVICE OF AN ORACLE, PELIAS SLAUGHTERED HIS FAMILY IN ORDER TO SAFEGUARD HIS RULE. ONLY MY FATHER, HIS HALF-BROTHER, SURVIVED.
I WAS RAISED IN COMPLETE IGNORANCE OF MY NOBLE BIRTH. ALL I KNEW WAS THAT KING PELIAS WAS HOLDING GAMES IN HONOR OF HIS FATHER, POSEIDON. I WANTED TO COMPETE IN THEM.
I SET OUT FOR THE GAMES, AND I CAME TO THE SHORE OF THE RIVER ANAUROS. IT WAS SPRING, AND THE RIVER HAD SWELLED UNDER THE RAIN AND MELTED SNOW.
THERE I MET AN OLD WOMAN, WHO ASKED ME TO CARRY HER ACROSS.
OF COURSE, I AGREED.
I GRADUALLY BECAME AWARE THAT THE OLD WOMAN HAD CHANGED.
SHE WAS BOTH HEAVIER AND LIGHTER AT THE SAME TIME, LIKE THE AIR ON A HOT SUMMER DAY.

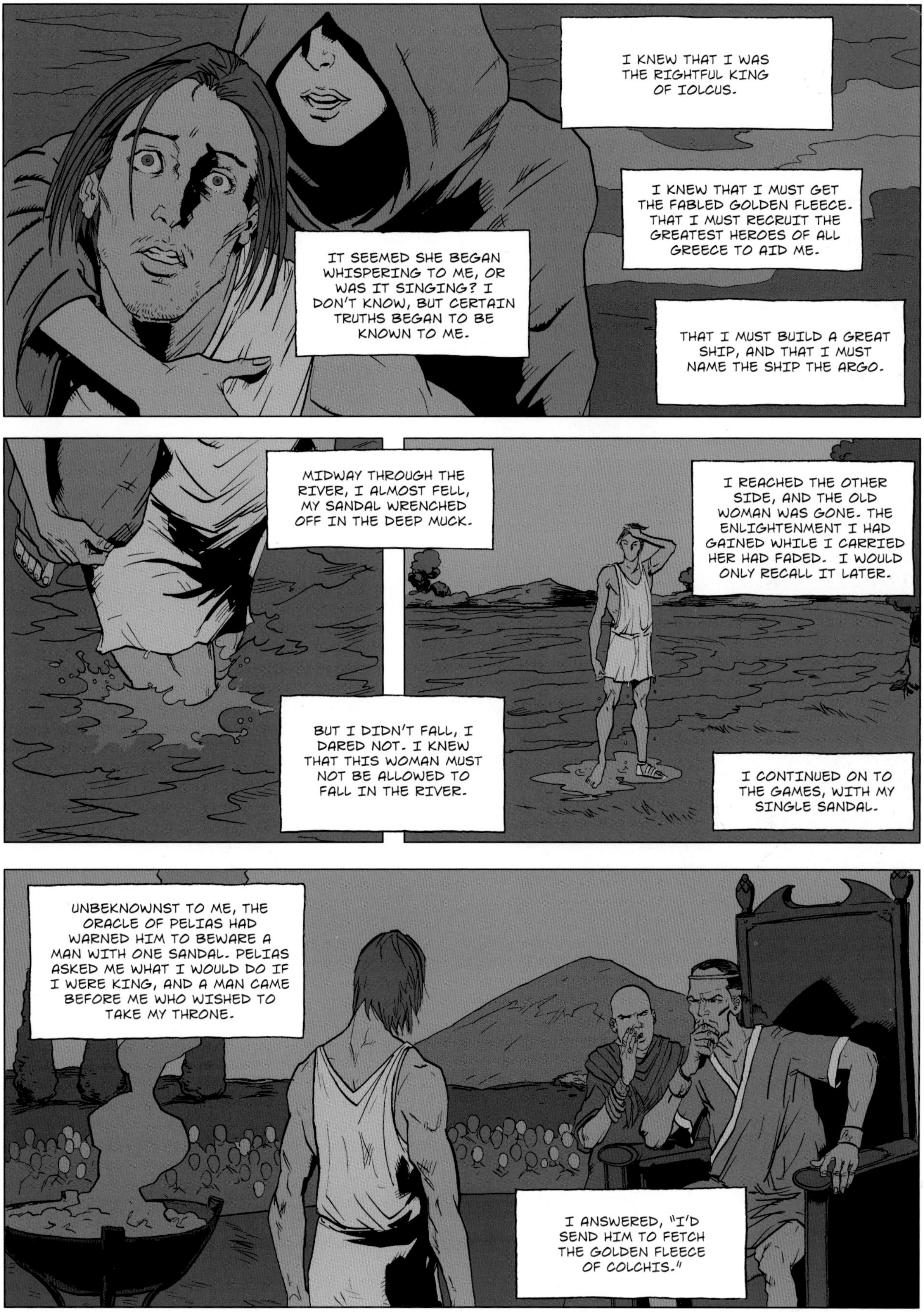
I KNEW THAT I WAS THE RIGHTFUL KING OF IOLCUS.
IT SEEMED SHE BEGAN WHISPERING TO ME, OR WAS IT SINGING? I DON'T KNOW, BUT CERTAIN TRUTHS BEGAN TO BE KNOWN TO ME.
I KNEW THAT I MUST GET THE FABLED GOLDEN FLEECE. THAT I MUST RECRUIT THE GREATEST HEROES OF ALL GREECE TO AID ME.
THAT I MUST BUILD A GREAT SHIP, AND THAT I MUST NAME THE SHIP THE ARGO.
MIDWAY THROUGH THE RIVER, I ALMOST FELL, MY SANDAL WRENCHED OFF IN THE DEEP MUCK.
BUT I DIDN'T FALL, I DARED NOT. I KNEW THAT THIS WOMAN MUST NOT BE ALLOWED TO FALL IN THE RIVER.
I REACHED THE OTHER SIDE, AND THE OLD WOMAN WAS GONE. THE ENLIGHTENMENT I HAD GAINED WHILE I CARRIED HER HAD FADED. I WOULD ONLY RECALL IT LATER.
I CONTINUED ON TO THE GAMES, WITH MY SINGLE SANDAL.
UNBEKNOWNST TO ME, THE ORACLE OF PELIAS HAD WARNED HIM TO BEWARE A MAN WITH ONE SANDAL. PELIAS ASKED ME WHAT I WOULD DO IF I WERE KING, AND A MAN CAME BEFORE ME WHO WISHED TO TAKE MY THRONE.
I ANSWERED, "I'D SEND HIM TO FETCH THE GOLDEN FLEECE OF COLCHIS."

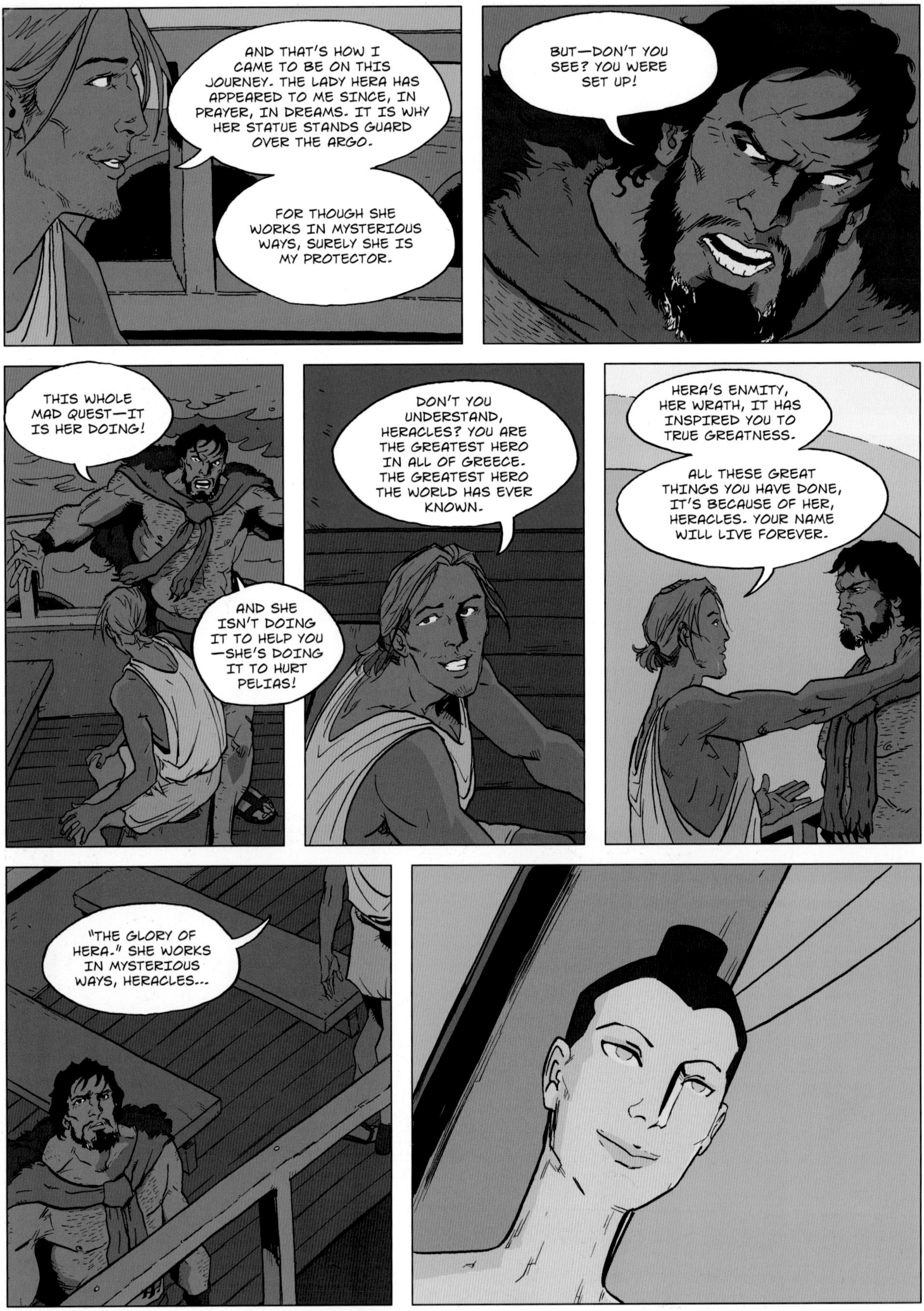
AND THAT'S HOW I CAME TO BE ON THIS JOURNEY. THE LADY HERA HAS APPEARED TO ME SINCE, IN PRAYER, IN DREAMS. IT IS WHY HER STATUE STANDS GUARD OVER THE ARGO.
FOR THOUGH SHE WORKS IN MYSTERIOUS WAYS, SURELY SHE IS MY PROTECTOR.
BUT—DON'T YOU SEE? YOU WERE SET UP!
THIS WHOLE MAD QUEST—IT IS HER DOING!
AND SHE ISN'T DOING IT TO HELP YOU —SHE'S DOING IT TO HURT PELIAS!
DON'T YOU UNDERSTAND, HERACLES? YOU ARE THE GREATEST HERO IN ALL OF GREECE. THE GREATEST HERO THE WORLD HAS EVER KNOWN.
HERA'S ENMITY, HER WRATH, IT HAS INSPIRED YOU TO TRUE GREATNESS.
ALL THESE GREAT THINGS YOU HAVE DONE, IT'S BECAUSE OF HER, HERACLES. YOUR NAME WILL LIVE FOREVER.
"THE GLORY OF HERA." SHE WORKS IN MYSTERIOUS WAYS, HERACLES...

UNFORTUNATELY, HERACLES WOULD NOT FINISH THE QUEST FOR THE GOLDEN FLEECE.

DURING HIS TIME ON THE ARGO, HERACLES MADE A PARTICULAR FRIENDSHIP WITH A YOUTH NAMED HYLAS.

IN MYSIA, HYLAS WENT ASHORE TO FETCH FRESH WATER FOR THE CREW. THERE HE RAN AFOUL OF SOME NYMPHS WHO WERE ENAMORED OF HIS YOUTHFUL BEAUTY, AND HYLAS WAS NEVER SEEN AGAIN.

UNABLE TO FIND HIS FAITHFUL COMPANION, HERACLES WENT INTO A RAGE, THREATENING TO DESTROY THE COUNTRY UNTIL HE DISCOVERED WHETHER HYLAS WAS DEAD OR ALIVE.

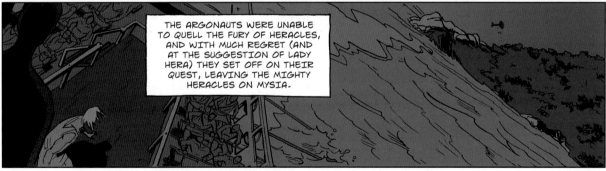

THE ARGONAUTS WERE UNABLE TO QUELL THE FURY OF HERACLES, AND WITH MUCH REGRET (AND AT THE SUGGESTION OF LADY HERA) THEY SET OFF ON THEIR QUEST, LEAVING THE MIGHTY HERACLES ON MYSIA.

AFTER A TIME, HERACLES RETURNED TO HIS SENSES, AND, GRIEVED AND SADDENED, HE SET OUT ONCE MORE, ALONE, TO FETCH THE APPLES OF THE HESPERIDES.

BUT HOW COULD ONE SUCH AS HE SAFELY ENTER THE MOST SECRET AND HOLY PRECINCT OF THE GODDESS HERA?

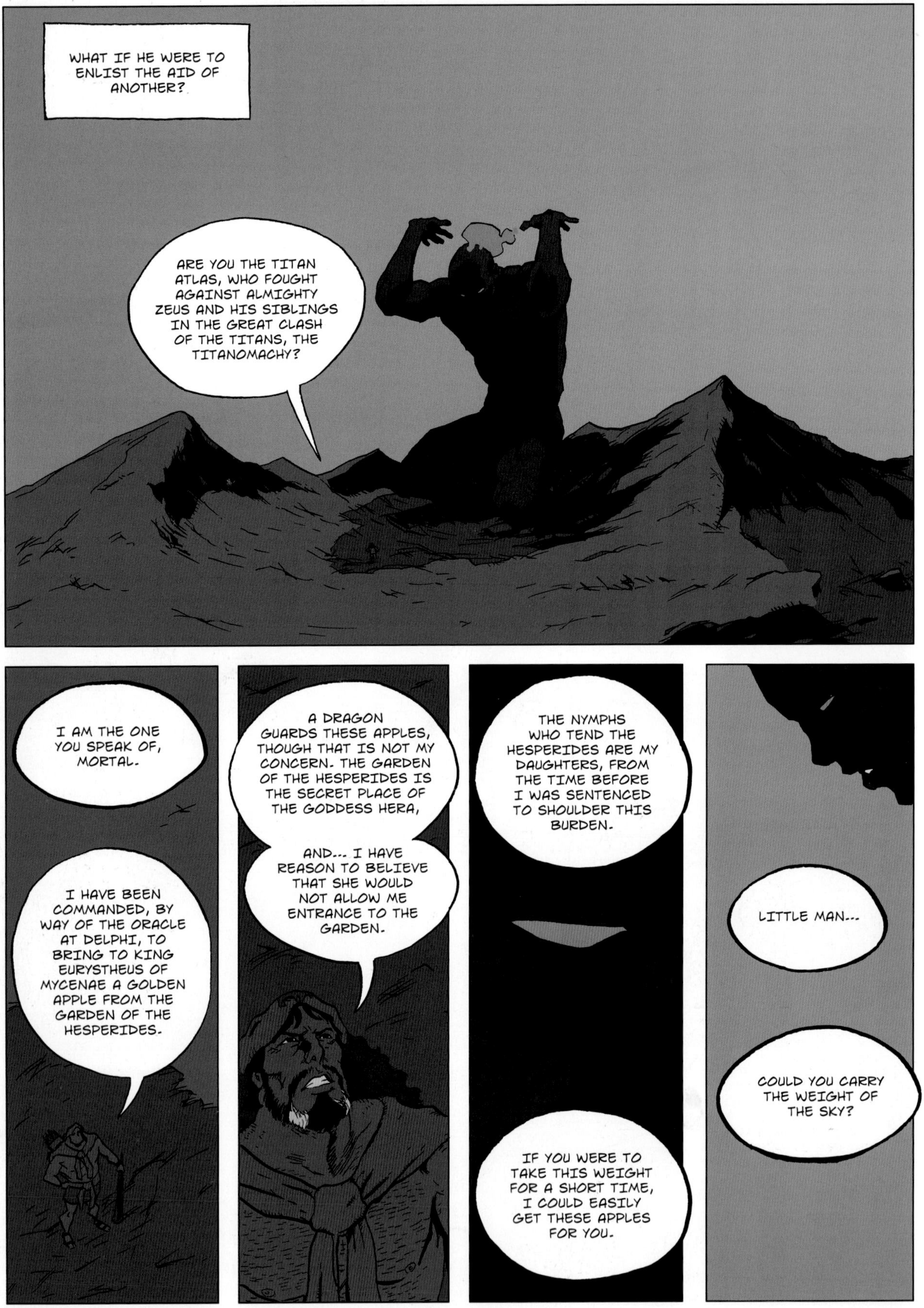
WHAT IF HE WERE TO ENLIST THE AID OF ANOTHER?
ARE YOU THE TITAN ATLAS, WHO FOUGHT AGAINST ALMIGHTY ZEUS AND HIS SIBLINGS IN THE GREAT CLASH OF THE TITANS, THE TITANOMACHY?
I AM THE ONE YOU SPEAK OF, MORTAL.
I HAVE BEEN COMMANDED, BY WAY OF THE ORACLE AT DELPHI, TO BRING TO KING EURYSTHEUS OF MYCENAE A GOLDEN APPLE FROM THE GARDEN OF THE HESPERIDES.
A DRAGON GUARDS THESE APPLES, THOUGH THAT IS NOT MY CONCERN. THE GARDEN OF THE HESPERIDES IS THE SECRET PLACE OF THE GODDESS HERA,
AND... I HAVE REASON TO BELIEVE THAT SHE WOULD NOT ALLOW ME ENTRANCE TO THE GARDEN.
THE NYMPHS WHO TEND THE HESPERIDES ARE MY DAUGHTERS, FROM THE TIME BEFORE I WAS SENTENCED TO SHOULDER THIS BURDEN.
IF YOU WERE TO TAKE THIS WEIGHT FOR A SHORT TIME, I COULD EASILY GET THESE APPLES FOR YOU.
LITTLE MAN...
COULD YOU CARRY THE WEIGHT OF THE SKY?

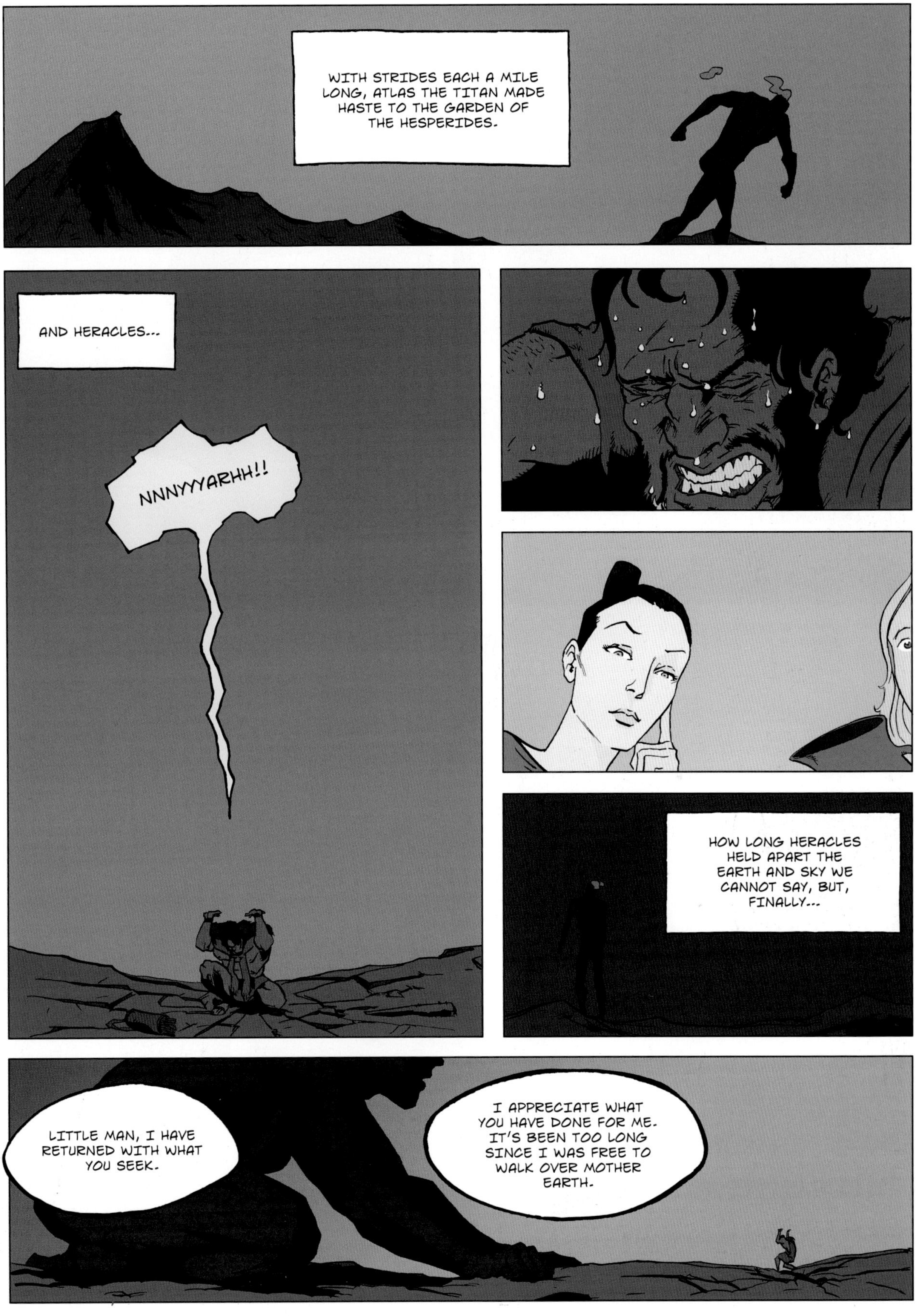
WITH STRIDES EACH A MILE LONG, ATLAS THE TITAN MADE HASTE TO THE GARDEN OF THE HESPERIDES.
AND HERACLES...
NNNYYYARHH!!
HOW LONG HERACLES HELD APART THE EARTH AND SKY WE CANNOT SAY, BUT, FINALLY...
LITTLE MAN, I HAVE RETURNED WITH WHAT YOU SEEK.
I APPRECIATE WHAT YOU HAVE DONE FOR ME. IT'S BEEN TOO LONG SINCE I WAS FREE TO WALK OVER MOTHER EARTH.

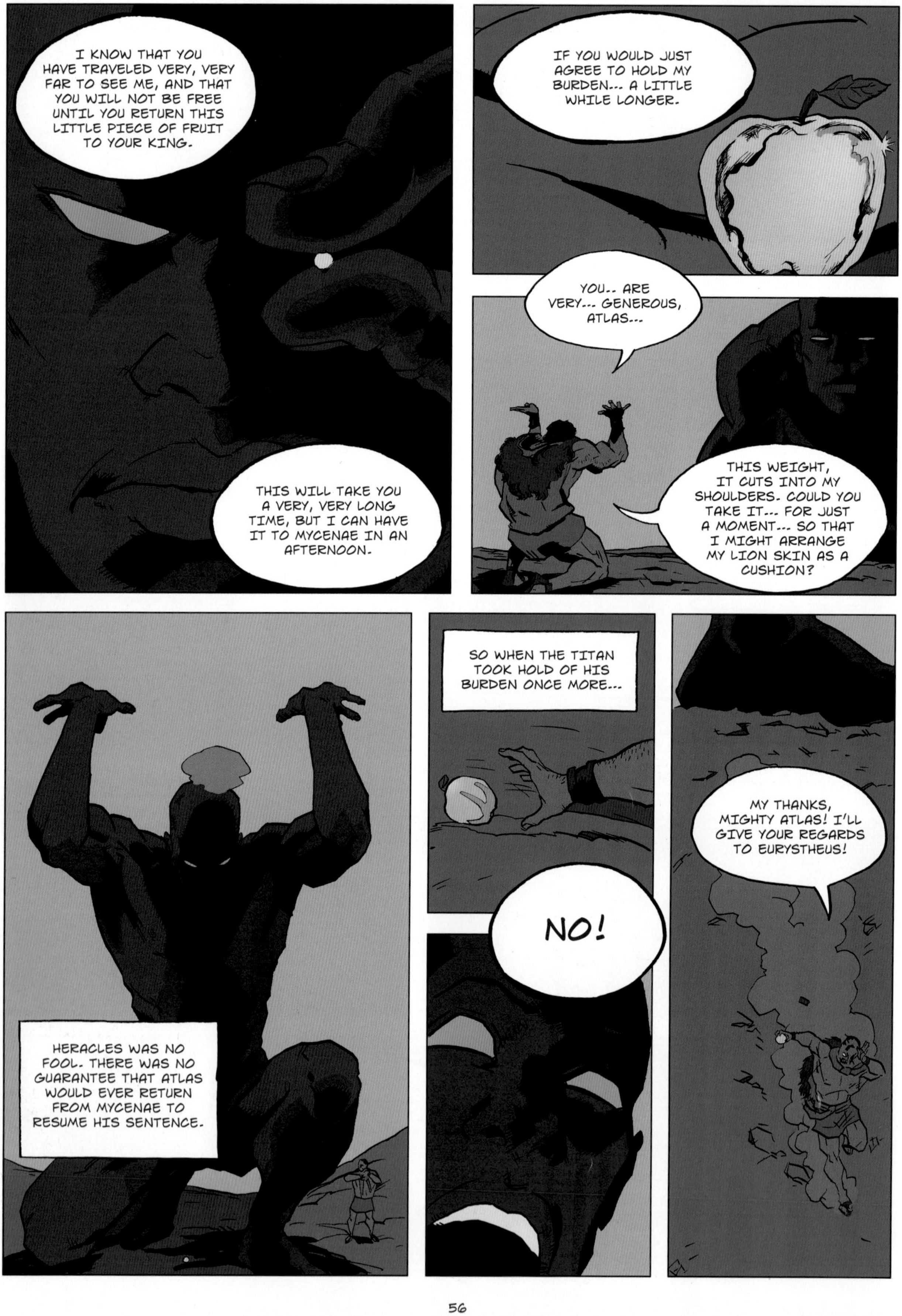
I KNOW THAT YOU HAVE TRAVELED VERY, VERY FAR TO SEE ME, AND THAT YOU WILL NOT BE FREE UNTIL YOU RETURN THIS LITTLE PIECE OF FRUIT TO YOUR KING.
THIS WILL TAKE YOU A VERY, VERY LONG TIME, BUT I CAN HAVE IT TO MYCENAE IN AN AFTERNOON.
IF YOU WOULD JUST AGREE TO HOLD MY BURDEN... A LITTLE WHILE LONGER.
YOU.. ARE VERY... GENEROUS, ATLAS...
THIS WEIGHT, IT CUTS INTO MY SHOULDERS. COULD YOU TAKE IT... FOR JUST A MOMENT... SO THAT I MIGHT ARRANGE MY LION SKIN AS A CUSHION?
HERACLES WAS NO FOOL. THERE WAS NO GUARANTEE THAT ATLAS WOULD EVER RETURN FROM MYCENAE TO RESUME HIS SENTENCE.
SO WHEN THE TITAN TOOK HOLD OF HIS BURDEN ONCE MORE...
NO!
MY THANKS, MIGHTY ATLAS! I'LL GIVE YOUR REGARDS TO EURYSTHEUS!

SIIIGH...

HE DID IT...

YOU DID IT!!

I SEND YOU TO FETCH AN APPLE FROM THE SACRED GARDEN OF YOUR MOST DEADLY ENEMY—

AND—SOMEHOW—YOU DID IT!!

TIME AND TIME AGAIN I SEND THIS MUSCLE-BOUND CLOD TO THE FAR CORNERS OF THE EARTH—

AND NO MATTER HOW IMPOSSIBLE THE TASK—HE DOES IT!

WELL, NO MORE! I CAN'T TAKE IT ANYMORE!

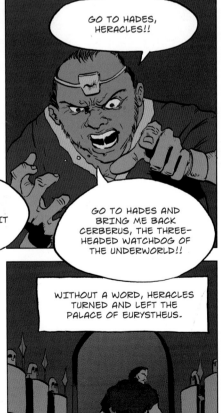

GO TO HADES, HERACLES!!

GO TO HADES AND BRING ME BACK CERBERUS, THE THREE-HEADED WATCHDOG OF THE UNDERWORLD!!

WITHOUT A WORD, HERACLES TURNED AND LEFT THE PALACE OF EURYSTHEUS.

AND THAT WAS THAT. FOR A LONG TIME, THAT WAS THE LAST ANYONE SAW OF HERACLES.

NO MORTAL COULD JOURNEY TO THE UNDERWORLD OF HADES AND RETURN. EVEN AMONG THE GODS, ONLY HERMES AND HADES HIMSELF COULD DO SO.

IT SEEMED HERACLES HAD FINALLY MET HIS END.

BUT THEN...

CERBERUS OBEYED NONE BUT HIS MASTER, HADES. AND SO, EVERY STEP OF THE WAY FROM THE UNDERWORLD, HERACLES FOUGHT, HE PULLED, HE STRAINED.

THE CLAWS OF CERBERUS DUG DEEP INTO THE EARTH. HIS THREE MOUTHS DRIPPED BOILING POISON. HIS SERPENT TAIL LASHED.

AND STILL, HERACLES CAME FORWARD. STEP. BY STEP.

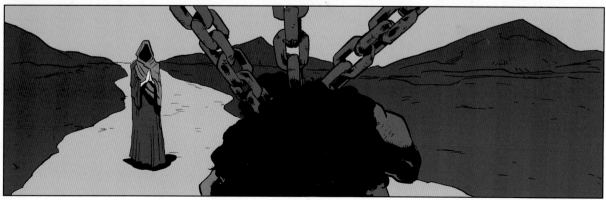

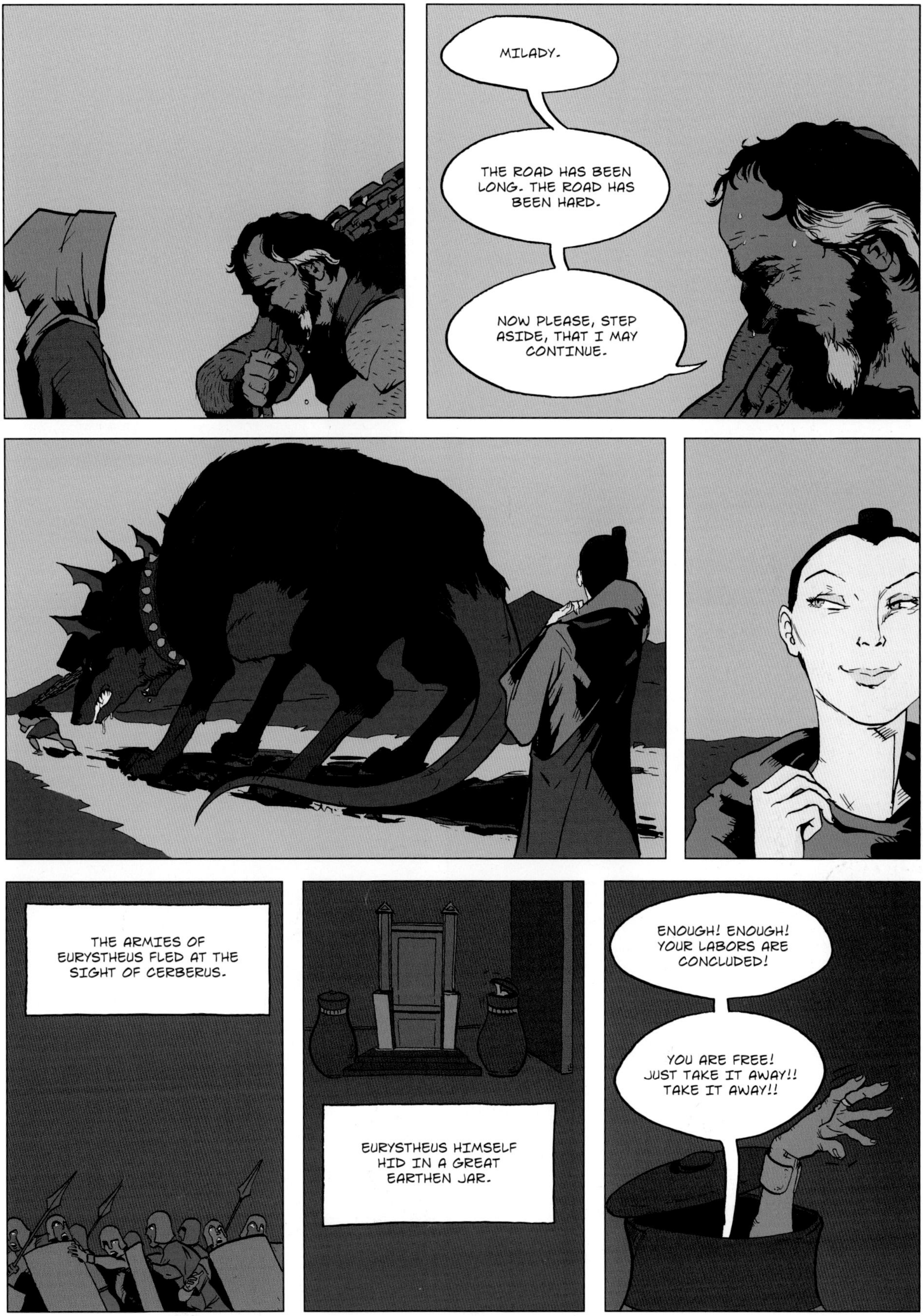
MILADY.
THE ROAD HAS BEEN LONG. THE ROAD HAS BEEN HARD.
NOW PLEASE, STEP ASIDE, THAT I MAY CONTINUE.
THE ARMIES OF EURYSTHEUS FLED AT THE SIGHT OF CERBERUS.
EURYSTHEUS HIMSELF HID IN A GREAT EARTHEN JAR.
ENOUGH! ENOUGH! YOUR LABORS ARE CONCLUDED!
YOU ARE FREE! JUST TAKE IT AWAY!! TAKE IT AWAY!!

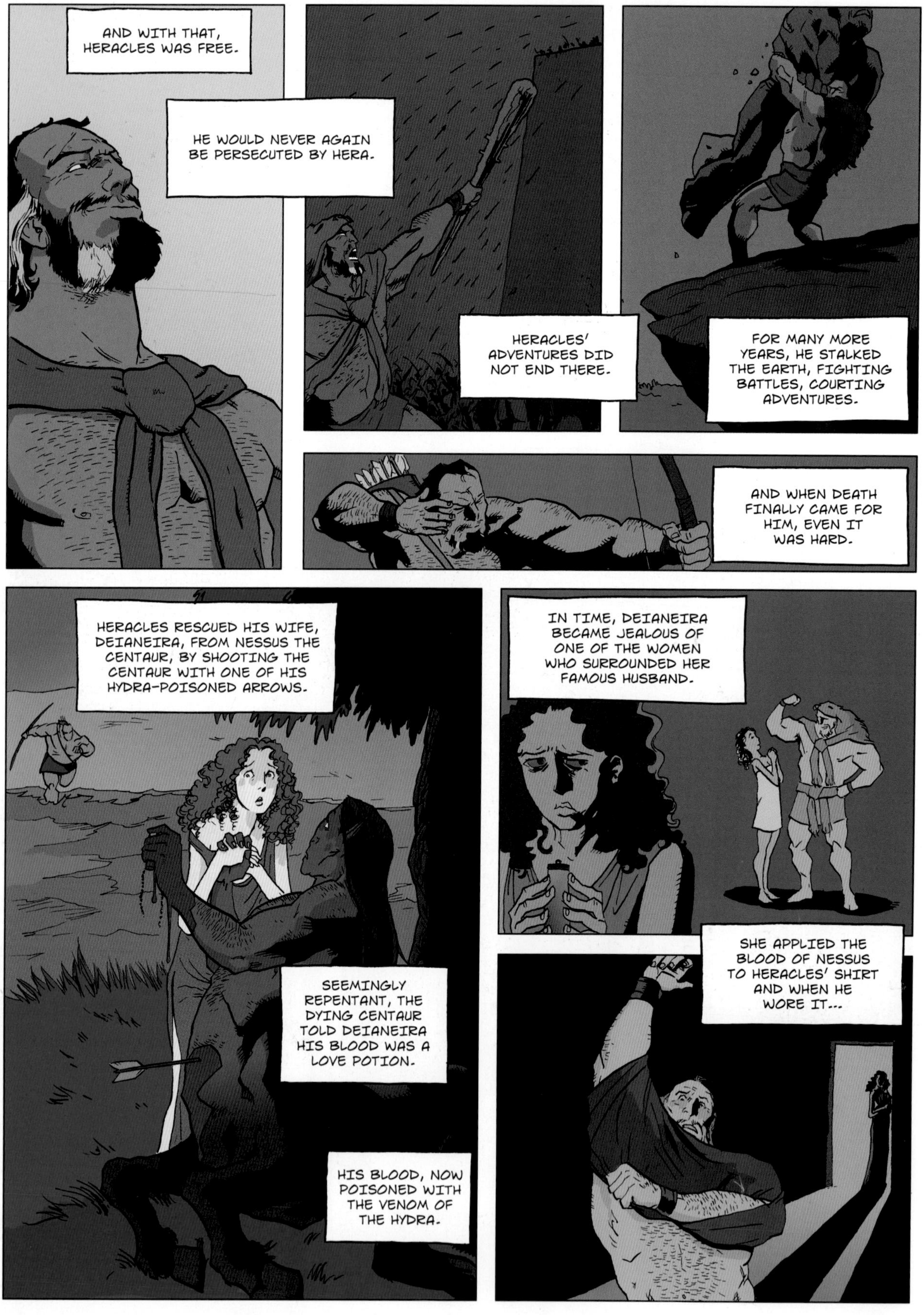
AND WITH THAT, HERACLES WAS FREE.
HE WOULD NEVER AGAIN BE PERSECUTED BY HERA.
HERACLES' ADVENTURES DID NOT END THERE.
FOR MANY MORE YEARS, HE STALKED THE EARTH, FIGHTING BATTLES, COURTING ADVENTURES.
AND WHEN DEATH FINALLY CAME FOR HIM, EVEN IT WAS HARD.
HERACLES RESCUED HIS WIFE, DEIANEIRA, FROM NESSUS THE CENTAUR, BY SHOOTING THE CENTAUR WITH ONE OF HIS HYDRA-POISONED ARROWS.
SEEMINGLY REPENTANT, THE DYING CENTAUR TOLD DEIANEIRA HIS BLOOD WAS A LOVE POTION.
HIS BLOOD, NOW POISONED WITH THE VENOM OF THE HYDRA.
IN TIME, DEIANEIRA BECAME JEALOUS OF ONE OF THE WOMEN WHO SURROUNDED HER FAMOUS HUSBAND.
SHE APPLIED THE BLOOD OF NESSUS TO HERACLES' SHIRT AND WHEN HE WORE IT...

THE POISON WRACKED HERACLES WITH UNBEARABLE PAIN. THERE WAS ONLY ONE WAY HE COULD ESCAPE IT.

HE CLIMBED ATOP A FUNERAL PYRE. IOLAUS, HIS FAITHFUL COMPANION FROM THE HYDRA ADVENTURE, RETURNED, NOW A FULL-GROWN MAN.

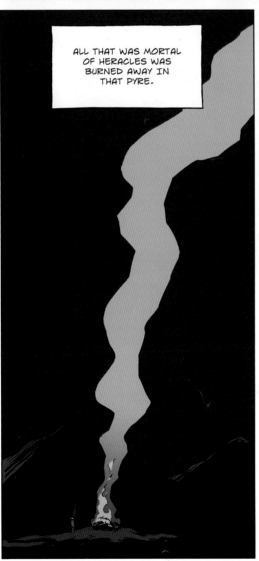

ALL THAT WAS MORTAL OF HERACLES WAS BURNED AWAY IN THAT PYRE.

THERE IS A STORY THEY TELL OF HERACLES...

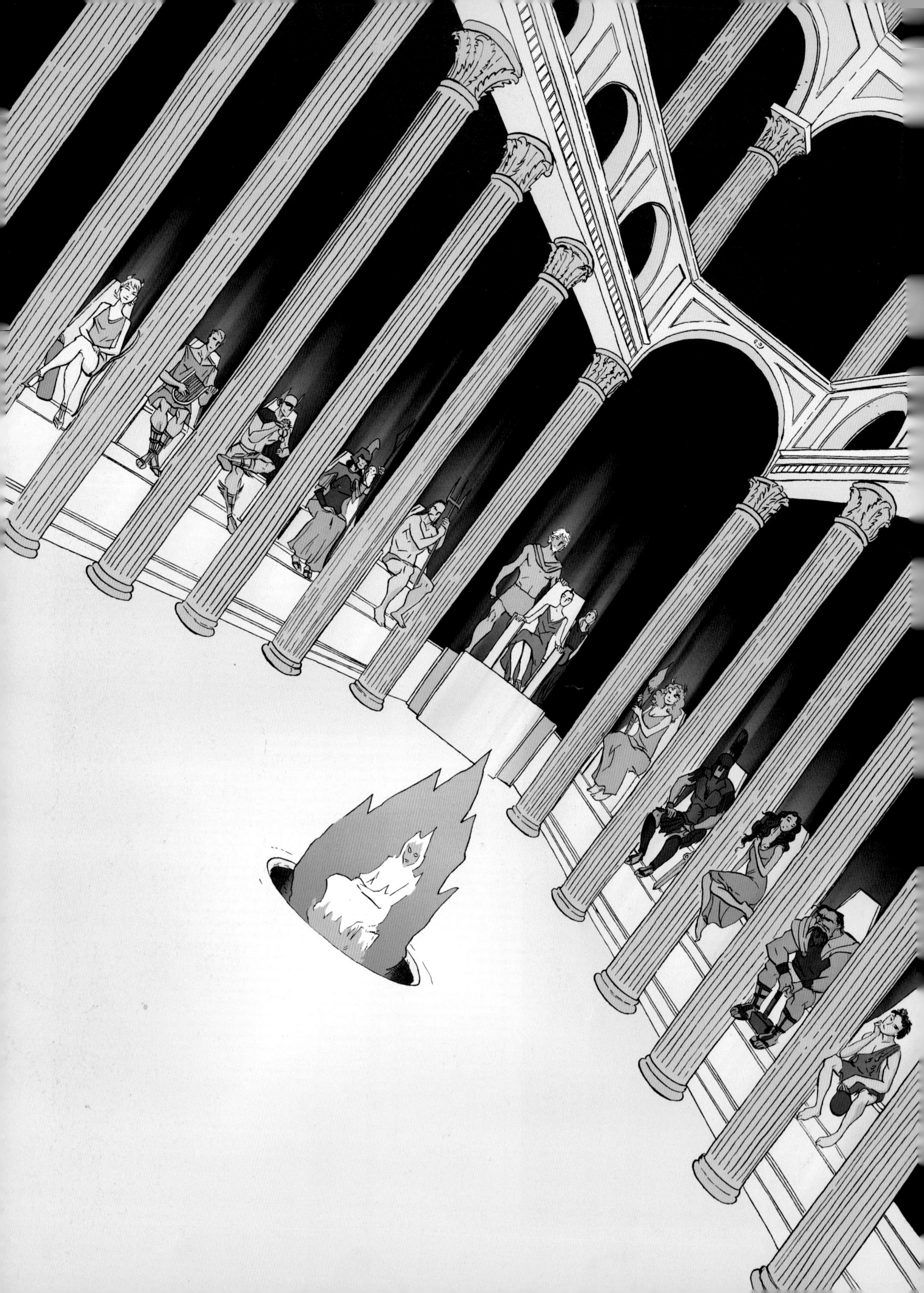

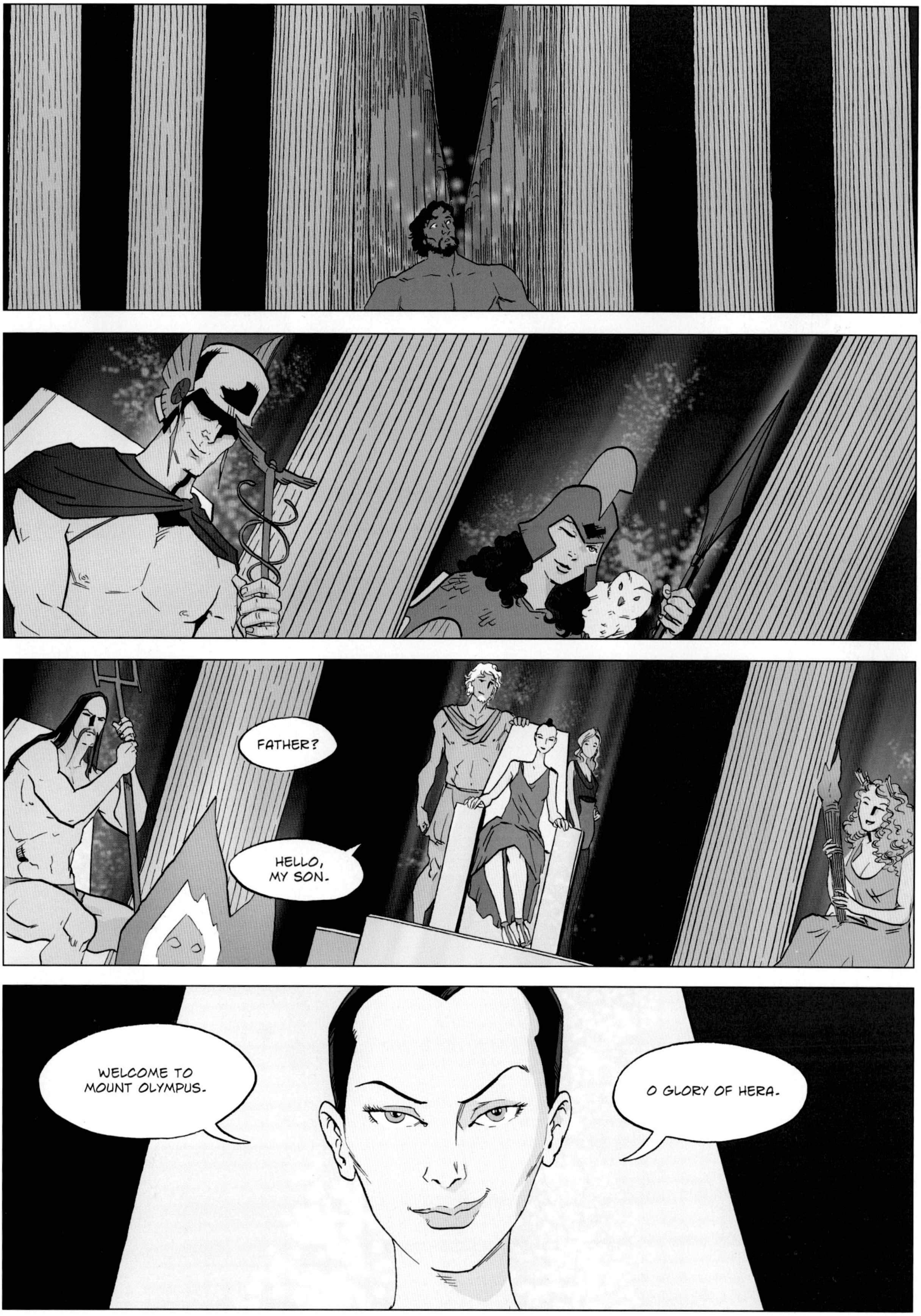
FATHER?
HELLO, MY SON.
WELCOME TO MOUNT OLYMPUS.
O GLORY OF HERA.

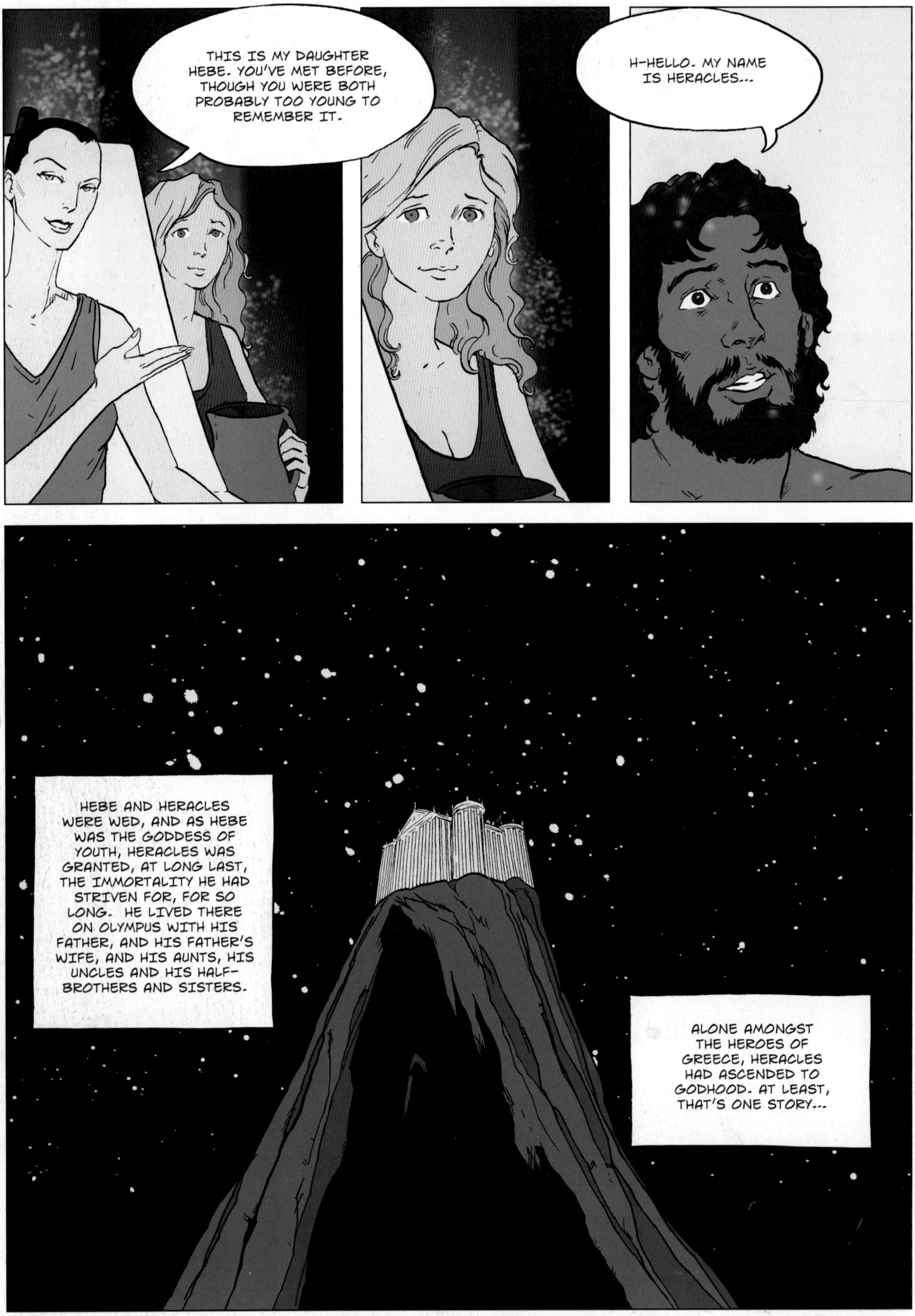
THIS IS MY DAUGHTER HEBE. YOU'VE MET BEFORE, THOUGH YOU WERE BOTH PROBABLY TOO YOUNG TO REMEMBER IT.
H-HELLO. MY NAME IS HERACLES...
HEBE AND HERACLES WERE WED, AND AS HEBE WAS THE GODDESS OF YOUTH, HERACLES WAS GRANTED, AT LONG LAST, THE IMMORTALITY HE HAD STRIVEN FOR, FOR SO LONG. HE LIVED THERE ON OLYMPUS WITH HIS FATHER, AND HIS FATHER'S WIFE, AND HIS AUNTS, HIS UNCLES AND HIS HALF-BROTHERS AND SISTERS.
ALONE AMONGST THE HEROES OF GREECE, HERACLES HAD ASCENDED TO GODHOOD. AT LEAST, THAT'S ONE STORY...

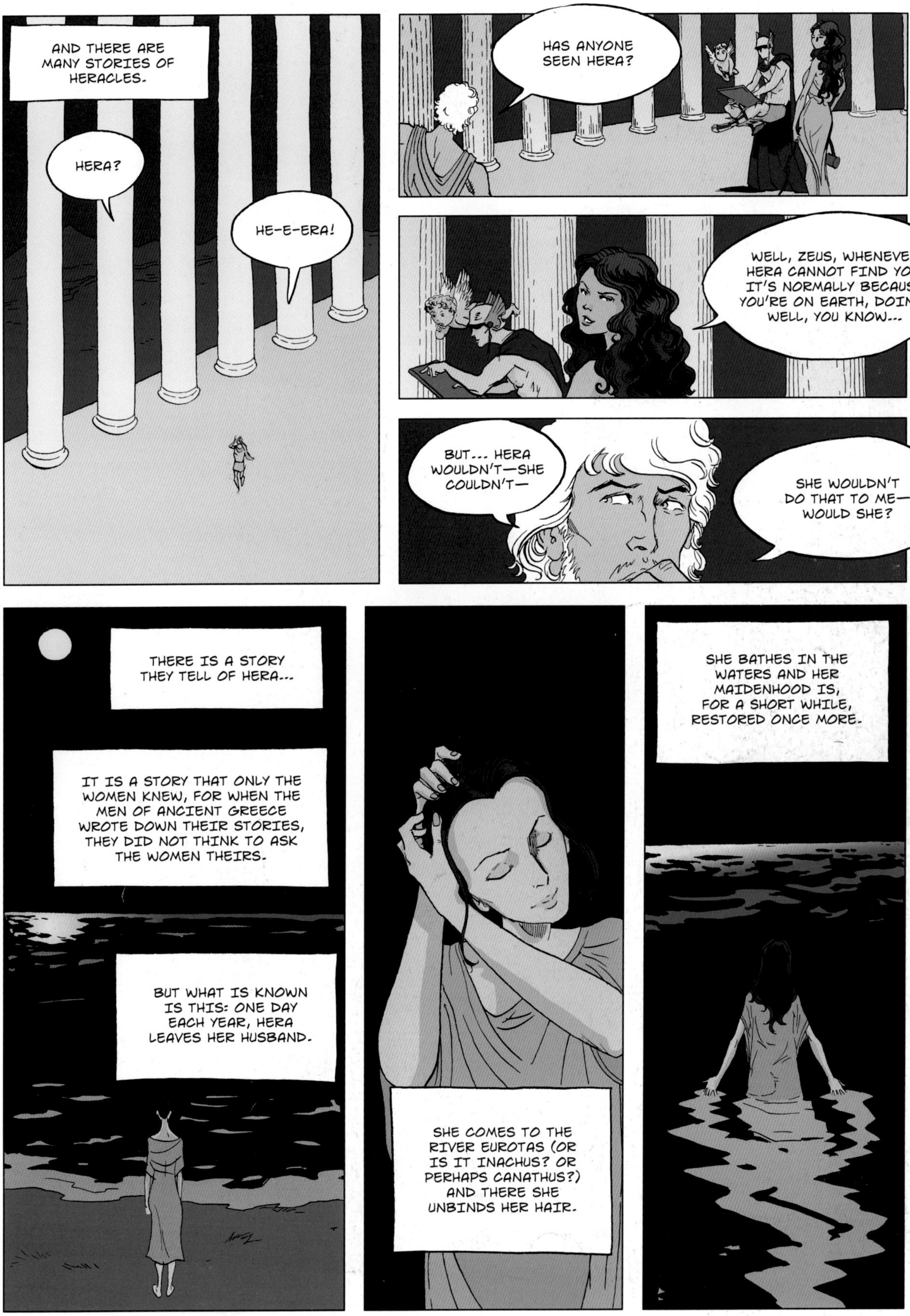
AND THERE ARE MANY STORIES OF HERACLES.
HERA?
HE-E-ERA!
HAS ANYONE SEEN HERA?
WELL, ZEUS, WHENEVER HERA CANNOT FIND YOU, IT'S NORMALLY BECAUSE YOU'RE ON EARTH, DOING, WELL, YOU KNOW...
BUT... HERA WOULDN'T—SHE COULDN'T—
SHE WOULDN'T DO THAT TO ME—WOULD SHE?
THERE IS A STORY THEY TELL OF HERA...
IT IS A STORY THAT ONLY THE WOMEN KNEW, FOR WHEN THE MEN OF ANCIENT GREECE WROTE DOWN THEIR STORIES, THEY DID NOT THINK TO ASK THE WOMEN THEIRS.
BUT WHAT IS KNOWN IS THIS: ONE DAY EACH YEAR, HERA LEAVES HER HUSBAND.
SHE COMES TO THE RIVER EUROTAS (OR IS IT INACHUS? OR PERHAPS CANATHUS?) AND THERE SHE UNBINDS HER HAIR.
SHE BATHES IN THE WATERS AND HER MAIDENHOOD IS, FOR A SHORT WHILE, RESTORED ONCE MORE.

FOR THAT ONE DAY,
AT LEAST, SHE IS NO
LONGER HERA, QUEEN
OF THE GODS.

NO LONGER HERA,
THE GODDESS OF
MARRIAGE.

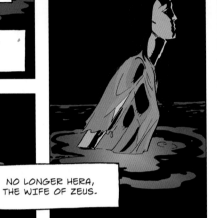

NO LONGER HERA,
THE WIFE OF ZEUS.

AND HOW DO YOU THINK
IT FEELS, TO BE HERA
ON THAT DAY?

GLORIOUS.

AUTHOR'S NOTE

Let me just state this up front—Hera is my favorite goddess. Part of it's because she's the one person that Zeus well and truly fears. Part of it is that I really like her style.

While working on OLYMPIANS, I noticed how, in modern society, the gods have become so... caricaturized. Hermes is always just "the messenger of the gods," no mention made of his myriad other functions. Hades is often depicted as a bad guy, because people have equated him with the devil. Hera is a shrew, a witch, a jealous wife.

Well, yeah, maybe that's true about Hera, but that's because *Zeus is a terrible husband*. He ate his first wife, for crying out loud. He's had dozens of children with his dozens of girlfriends—and then he has some of those children live with him on Olympus. With Hera. So Hera is jealous and punishes these girlfriends and children? Well, I say, really, who can blame her?

In preparation for OLYMPIANS, I spent some months traveling around Europe, visiting museums and ancient sites, taking photos and notes, basically trying to get a feel for the Greek gods on their home turf. I noticed that, at many sites, the oldest temple there would be Hera's. At many of them, the second oldest temple would be Hera's as well. Obviously, the people who built these temples saw her as something beyond just Zeus's jealous wife.

I also became aware that there was an alternate thread running through the myths, traces and remnants of stories older than the more familiar ones we know. Why was Heracles "the Glory of Hera"? Was it really just a transparent and unsuccessful attempt by his mother, Alcmene, to pacify the jealous goddess, as later writers speculated, or at one point in his history was he actually regarded as a champion of Greece's preeminent goddess? And what of the myth of the creation of the Milky Way, Hera's suckling of the infant Heracles? Or his marrying Hera's daughter Hebe upon ascending to Olympus? Strange behavior for such hated enemies, to be sure. I wrote in the text of this book that "when the men of ancient Greece wrote down their stories, they did not think to ask the women theirs," and this is true. The stories that were recorded were definitely

Several times during the creation of this book I jokingly told friends that my work was "the Hera Reclamation Project." Nothing is fabricated here—all of the stories I tell are out there, and they're not that hard to find. I just cast some light on versions of the stories that tend to get a little less attention than others. In particular, and largely because I wanted to include the creation myth of the Milky Way, I left out the well-known story of Heracles's murdering of his own children, because of a madness visited upon him by Hera. The added bonus was that it rescued both characters—the murdering of innocent children is a heavy deed, one that weighs down both Heracles and Hera in unrelenting tragedy and contemptibility. Coupled with the parable of Heracles before the forked road, I felt the idea of Heracles proving his worthiness to ascend to Olympus as Zeus's son rather than the redemption of a murderer to be the road best taken.

So please, sit back, read, and enjoy this take on the Queen of the Gods. Let it settle in, and imagine, if you will, how the people of ancient Greece might have pictured their most important goddess. Maybe Hera will become your favorite goddess too. There's just something about her style...

George O'Connor
Brooklyn, NY
2011

the men's tales. The women of Greece had their own stories that mothers would pass down to daughters. This was highly classified information—women only. Hints of these tales survive, in art, in descriptions of festivals, and in ancient rites. Occasionally, a fragment or two of myth makes it into the writings. But by and large, the women's stories are lost to us, leaving only these tantalizing glimpses of another facet of the ancient Greeks' beliefs. Maybe one of those lost tales tells how Hera really felt about Heracles.

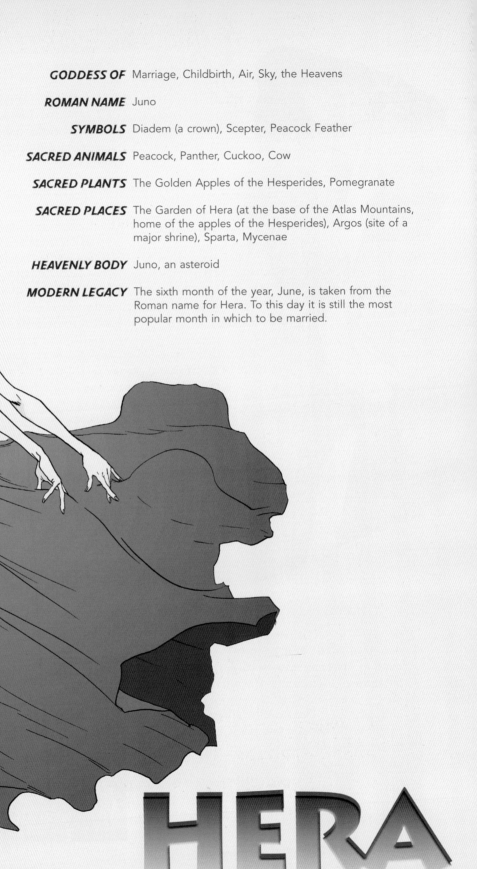

GODDESS OF	Marriage, Childbirth, Air, Sky, the Heavens
ROMAN NAME	Juno
SYMBOLS	Diadem (a crown), Scepter, Peacock Feather
SACRED ANIMALS	Peacock, Panther, Cuckoo, Cow
SACRED PLANTS	The Golden Apples of the Hesperides, Pomegranate
SACRED PLACES	The Garden of Hera (at the base of the Atlas Mountains, home of the apples of the Hesperides), Argos (site of a major shrine), Sparta, Mycenae
HEAVENLY BODY	Juno, an asteroid
MODERN LEGACY	The sixth month of the year, June, is taken from the Roman name for Hera. To this day it is still the most popular month in which to be married.

HERA
QUEEN OF THE GODS

GⱭEEK NOTES

PAGE 3: We saw more of the gigantomachy, or the war of the giants, in OLYMPIANS BOOK 2: ATHENA: GREY-EYED GODDESS.

PAGE 4, PANEL 1: A reference to the events of OLYMPIANS BOOK 1: ZEUS: KING OF THE GODS

PAGE 4, PANEL 3: Another scene from ATHENA. Now you know what Hera and Demeter were whispering.

PAGE 4, PANEL 5: Metis disappeared because Zeus ate her. She lived in his head, where she gave birth to his daughter Athena. Zeus doesn't know about that at this point—he just thinks he has a headache. Once again, see ATHENA for more details.

PAGE 5, PANEL 5: These are some of Zeus's many loves before Hera. He had divine offspring with most of them.

PAGE 8, PANEL 1: Zeus takes the form of a cuckoo bird here in order to trick Hera into allowing him into her room. The cuckoo is a bird known for leaving its eggs in other birds' nests, and tricking them into raising the cuckoo's offspring.

PAGE 9, PANEL 2: As the goddess of marriage, it makes sense that Hera would make such a distinction between a wife and a queen.

PAGE 9, PANEL 4: Among the attendees of the wedding of Zeus and Hera we see the Titanesses and Oceanus (who did not side with the Titans in the titanomachy). The three Fates are presiding over the ceremony, and since it's occurring during the day, Helios is in attendance, but not poor Selene. Hopefully she had fun later at the reception.

PAGE 11, PANEL 3: This dragon, Ladon, is a child of Typhon and Echidna, and we meet some of his siblings later in the story.

PAGE 13, PANEL 5: The nine women pictured with Apollo here are the Muses, the goddesses of poetry, song, and dance. We'll learn a lot more about them in Apollo's book.

PAGE 14, PANELS 5, 6: In addition to her duties as queen of the gods and the goddess of marriage, Hera was the goddess of the air and sky, hence the way she descends to Earth.

PAGE 16, PANEL 3: "Cow-eyed." It may sound as if Zeus has put his foot so far into his mouth that he's swallowed his own leg, but, believe it or not, "Boopis" (meaning "cow-eyed") was a very common epithet for Hera. Apparently the ancient Greeks thought that calling someone cow-eyed was a great compliment. I don't recommend trying that one nowadays.

PAGE 18, PANEL 1: Another reference to Hera's role as goddess of the sky.

PAGE 19: Poor Io. We will see much more about her, and her guardian, in later volumes of OLYMPIANS.

PAGE 20, PANEL 3: Hera cursed Leto to not be able to give birth anywhere on dry land. Watch future volumes of OLYMPIANS for her story.

PAGE 20, PANEL 4: Callisto was a nymph of Artemis's who, in some versions of her story, was transformed by Hera into a bear for having an affair with Zeus.

PAGE 20, PANEL 5: Some sources allege that Hera sent a madness upon Dionysos that set him wandering through Egypt for years. Other sources might contend that Dionysos didn't need the help, as he was crazy enough already.

PAGE 23, PANEL 1: That's Perseus rescuing Andromeda from the sea monster Cetus, as seen in ATHENA. The Greeks believed their children, in addition to founding the Greek kingdom of Mycenae, also went on to found the Persian Empire.

PAGE 23, PANEL 3: Zeus uses this trick more than once, as in the instance of Castor and Polydeuces, whom we meet later in this story.

PAGE 26, PANEL 2: As a virgin goddess, Athena is a little squeamish around children.

PAGE 26, PANEL 7: Hebe, goddess of youth, is a daughter of Zeus and Hera. Not considered one of the great gods (surprising, considering her pedigree), she nonetheless lived on Olympus and functioned as a cupbearer to the big twelve.

PAGE 27, PANEL 2: Remember the guardian of Io I mentioned earlier?

PAGE 28: I would be remiss if I didn't mention another tradition of why Heracles performs his Twelve Labors—as penance for murdering his own children after Hera makes him temporarily insane. I talk more about this decision in my Author's Note.

PAGE 28, PANEL 5: Wait a minute! Ten Labors? Wasn't it twelve? Well, the original deal was ten, but Eurysthenes demanded a redo for two of them.

PAGE 29, PANEL 1: Want to know how geeky I am? That's the actual Milky Way—what's more, it's during the meteor shower of the Perseids—"Perseids" means "children of Perseus," of which, several generations removed, Heracles is.

PAGE 34, PANEL 6: Sometimes I write a little something that gives me the giggles. Heracles' "oh yeah" after his third attempt to pierce the unbreakable skin of the Nemean Lion is one of those.

PAGE 41, PANEL 4: Hera's laughing because she knows how Heracles' story ends. Poisoning those arrows turns out to be a very fateful act.

PAGE 42, PANEL 4: Don't worry, Artemis! Heracles lets the stag go, it's fine!

PAGE 42, PANEL 8: Because I know someone will ask this, Heracles collects his poison arrows after each use. The venom is so deadly that they can be used again and again.

PAGE 45, PANEL 4: More on this bull in Poseidon's book.

PAGE 46: Hippolyte is the mother of the superhero Wonder Woman. Also look carefully in panel 2 to see Hera stirring up trouble for our boy Heracles.

PAGE 48, PANEL 1: In ancient Greece, athletes would perform in the nude. That means those guys running are actually naked. Point and laugh, kids, point and laugh.

PAGE 48: More on Jason and the Argonauts in later volumes of OLYMPIANS.

PAGE 52, PANEL 7: My inclusion of the statue of Hera at the mast is a little nod to the classic 1963 film JASON AND THE ARGONAUTS. You should see it if you haven't already.

PAGE 54, PANEL 5: It's the sky! How heavy could it be? Well, according to the National Center for Atmospheric Research, the atmosphere of the Earth weighs approximately 5 quadrillion (that's 5 with 15 zeroes after it) metric tons. So, I feel pretty confident in saying that, no, I couldn't carry the weight of the sky. How about you?

PAGE 57, PANEL 1: Man, Atlas, I can't believe you fell for that. Once again, point and laugh, kids.

PAGE 59, PANEL 7: Strangely enough, the image of Eurytheus hiding in giant jars from the monsters Heracles brought to him was extremely popular in ancient art.

PAGE 60, PANEL 2: That's Heracles storming the city of Troy (years before the Trojan War).

PAGE 60, PANEL 3: Heracles fighting the Gigante Antaeus. Special thanks to Dean Haspiel for the design of Antaeus.

PAGE 61: Among the ancients, the story of the ascendance of Heracles to Olympus was a controversial one. According to some, upon his death, Heracles became a god, as depicted here. Yet, in the *Odyssey*, Odysseus encounters and converses with the ghost of Heracles in Hades. Some people decided that the mortal side of Heracles was a ghost in Hades, whereas the immortal side resided on Olympus, effectively creating two different Heracleses. In cult, Heracles was venerated both as a god and as a hero.

PAGE 62: Left to right, we have: Artemis, Apollo, Hermes, Athena, Poseidon, Zeus, Hera, Hebe, Demeter, Ares, Aphrodite, Hephaistos, and Dionysos. Hestia has her customary spot at the hearth, in the center.

PAGE 63, PANEL 3: Hera is frequently depicted seated at her throne, with Zeus standing beside her, in ancient Greek statuary. Sometimes Zeus would be depicted in the form of the cuckoo he used to seduce her.

PAGE 64: That's the actual constellation Hercules visible behind Olympus.

PAGE 65, PANELS 2, 3: Hermes is depicted teaching Aphrodite's son Eros how to read. It's a nod to one of my favorite paintings, Corregio's *The Education of Cupid*. You should look it up, it's pretty.

PAGE 65: This is true about the men of ancient Greece. Most of the traditions we know of are men's traditions—it's one of the reasons why Hera has such a bad rep. The worshippers of Heracles in particular were very sexist, and didn't allow women into their temples. The different sites for Hera's rebirth as a maiden are all correct, by the way. Her annual renewal was a rite practiced at many locations by women throughout the ancient world. As the preeminent goddess, Hera symbolized women at the three stages of their lives—maiden, wife, and widow. As an ageless goddess, she went through the cycle every year, leaving her husband and starting all over again.

ABOUT THIS BOOK

HERA: THE GODDESS AND HER GLORY is the third book in OLYMPIANS, a new graphic novel series from First Second that retells the Greek myths.

FOR DISCUSSION

1 Hera is the goddess of marriage, yet her own marriage to Zeus is full of fights. Who do you think is to blame for that, Zeus or Hera? (Watch out for lightning bolts and giant snakes when answering this question.)

2 When Jerry Siegel and Joe Shuster created Superman in the 1930's, they consciously modeled him on Heracles. What are some aspects that Superman and Heracles have in common?

3 Heracles and Jason are two of the greatest heroes of ancient Greece, and are both closely connected to Hera, but their respective relationships with her are quite different. Why do you think that is?

4 Many of the names in this book will be very familiar to modern readers, like Atlas and Heracles. What are some modern things that have names taken from Greek mythology?

5 Do you think it's fair that Hera punishes the children and girlfriends of Zeus? Is it fair that Zeus keeps cheating on Hera?

6 The number twelve comes up often in the Greek myths. Heracles performs twelve labors, there are twelve Olympians, and twelve Titans before them. Why is the number twelve so important? What other numbers come up a lot in the Greek myths?

7 Heracles is given a choice between a hard life, in which he would have to work for everything but would be remembered forever, and an easy life, in which everything would be given to him. Did he make the right choice? What would you choose?

8 Very few people believe in the Greek gods today. Why do you think it is important that we still learn about them?

BIRTH NAME	Alcides
ROMAN NAME	Hercules
SYMBOLS	Lion Skin, Olive Club, Golden Apple
SACRED PLACES	Thebes (place of birth), Argos (seat of his royal family), Nemea, Lerna, Elis, Ceryneia, Lake Stymphalos, Mount Eurymanthus, Thrace, Crete (sites of his labors), the Pillars of Heracles (the Straits of Gibraltar, erected by Heracles as the westernmost point of his travels)
HEAVENLY BODY	Hercules, a constellation
MODERN LEGACY	Heracles, more commonly known by his Roman name Hercules, to this day remains one of the most famous heroes of all time. He has starred in television series, movies, cartoons, comic books, video games, and virtually any form of entertainment you can think of. A very strong man may still be referred to as Hercules.

HERACLES
THE GLORY OF HERA

BIBLIOGRAPHY

PAUSANIAS. DESCRIPTION OF GREECE, VOLUME I: BOOKS 1–2. NEW YORK: LOEB CLASSICAL LIBRARY, 1918.

Pausanias was an ancient Greek writer from the 2nd century AD who traveled throughout the ancient world, visiting many already ancient sites and recording what he saw in what could be called the world's first travel guide. Mythologically speaking, he is very interesting because of the many myths and stories that would be otherwise lost that he records in his descriptions of statuary and temples. For instance, the only place I was able to find the story of Hera and the cuckoo was in this book. There are several volumes of his writings—this is merely the first.

THEOI GREEK MYTHOLOGY WEB SITE. WWW.THEOI.COM

Without a doubt, the single most valuable resource I came across in this entire venture. At theoi.com, you can find an encyclopedia of various gods and goddesses from Greek mythology, cross referenced with every mention of them they could find in literally hundreds of ancient Greek and Roman texts. Unfortunately, it's not quite complete, and it doesn't seem to be updated anymore.

MYTH INDEX WEB SITE WWW.MYTHINDEX.COM

Another mythology web site connected to Theoi.com. While it doesn't have the painstakingly compiled quotations of ancient texts, it does offer some amazing encyclopedic entries of virtually every character to ever pass through a Greek Myth. Pretty amazing.

ALSO RECOMMENDED
FOR YOUNGER READERS

D'Aulaires' Book of Greek Myths. Ingri and Edgar Parin D'Aulaire. New York: Doubleday, 1962.

Black Ships Before Troy. Rosemary Sutcliff and Alan Lee. London: Francis Lincoln, 2005.

Wanderings of Odysseus. Rosemary Sutcliff and Alan Lee. London: Francis Lincoln, 2005.

Young Zeus. G. Brian Karas. New York: Scholastic, 2010.

We Goddesses: Athena, Aphrodite, Hera. Doris Orgel, illustrated by Marilee Heyer. New York: DK Publishing, 1999.

FOR OLDER READERS

The Marriage of Cadmus and Harmony. Robert Calasso. New York: Knopf, 1993.

Mythology. Edith Hamilton. New York: Grand Central Publishing, 1999.

The HYDRA

NAME TRANSLATION "Water Serpent"

SACRED PLACE Lerna

HEAVENLY BODY Hydra, the largest constellation. Also Hydra, a moon in orbit around Pluto

MODERN LEGACY The Hydra lends her name to a genus of simple saltwater organisms with multiple tentacles, like heads, and the ability to regenerate itself into new organisms when cut apart.

In Marvel Comics, HYDRA is the name of a criminal organization. When apprehended, its members cry, "Cut off a limb and two more shall take its place!"

For Mom.
– G.O.

First Second

New York & London

Copyright © 2011 by George O'Connor

A Neal Porter Book
Published by First Second
First Second is an imprint of Roaring Brook Press,
a division of Holtzbrinck Publishing Holdings Limited Partnership
175 Fifth Avenue, New York, New York 10010

Distributed in the United Kingdom by Macmillan Children's Books,
a division of Pan Macmillan.

Cataloging-in-Publication Data is on file at the Library of Congress

Paperback ISBN: 978-1-59643-433-2
Hardcover ISBN: 978-1-59643-724-1

First Second books are available for special promotions and premiums.
For details, contact: Director of Special Markets, Holtzbrinck Publishers.

First Edition 2011

Cover design by Mark Siegel and Colleen AF Venable
Book design by Colleen AF Venable and Danica Novgorodoff

Printed in China by Macmillan Production (Asia) Ltd.,
Kwun Tong, Kowloon, Hong Kong (supplier code 10)

10 9 8 7 6 5 4 3 2